THE WIDOW OF REDBRIAR

Melinda Wyers

THANK YOU

To Traci, for reading all the early drafts. To my husband, who kept this from becoming a ghost story, and everyone else who sent words of encouragement.

Editing by Anima Editing
ISBN 978-1-7335707-1-8
Misprints Publishing
www.misprintspublishing.com

1

Welcome to Redbriar

Mary Ellen stepped off the soggy wooden deck of the ship as it slowly lurched against the edge of the pier. She walked quickly across the long, wet platform to where her mother and brothers, Tucker and Robert, were standing. A man dressed in a very thin, checkered suit and a tall, brown hat met them at the port, tipping his hat as he addressed them. He had the same English accent as Mary Ellen's mother—a little stronger maybe, given her mother's time in the States. Mary Ellen eventually caught his name during the rapid-fire conversation between him and her mother. His name was Edmund and he was one of the uncles that she had never met before, not that she had really heard from any of them back home in Georgia. They continued down the boardwalk and on toward town, her uncle's footmen rolling a cart of their belongings along behind them. Edmund brought them to a small tea room to eat while their trunks and cases were taken to the train station.

At the tea house, her brothers, tired from the trip, kicked each other under the table. Her uncle tapped his bony knuckles on the tabletop, and from the sound, she feared his bones would crack it. Tucker and Robert sat up bolt straight and continued eating their soup. Mary Ellen ate hers slowly, not quite sure what was in it. She assumed it was fish but couldn't interrupt her mother's conversation to ask. Robert picked up a nugget of the meat from the slippery green soup. "What is this, Momma?"

Her mother lowered his hand and told him it was eel.

"What'er eels?" he whispered to Mary Ellen.

She leaned over and whispered back, "It's kind of like a snake."

Robert dropped the chunk of meat back into his soup and pushed the bowl away. Tucker, meanwhile, thought the idea of snake soup was the best thing he had ever heard, and fished out the bits with his fingers, gobbling them up.

Her mother and uncle continued their conversation about the days when they were younger, and how much the house at Redbriar hadn't changed. She had been younger than Mary Ellen when she moved to Georgia nearly thirty years ago. They talked on and on about how the village had changed, who had married who, and all the other things that never quite made it into a letter.

A waiter came by and placed a small cup of hot coffee in front of each of them. Her uncle smiled. "You said in the last letter how much you missed it." Mary Ellen hadn't had coffee since the war started, the price of it having gone up to an unholy fifty dollars a pound. She took a slow sip, savoring the flavor—not cut with sweet potato peels or chicory, but proper coffee. Her uncle put a few cubes of sugar in his cup and mechanically stirred. "I made sure to stock some at Redbriar as well."

After their tea, they headed to the train station. Edmund had called for a coach to take them rather than making them walk, as it was much further than the tea house was from the docks. Mary Ellen looked out the open window of the coach, staring in wonder at just how many people were walking the streets. Stores lined the narrow cobblestone and were so small and neatly arranged that she couldn't tell where one ended and the next began. From what she understood from her father, London was supposed to be a "dirty shithole with a whorehouse on every corner." She didn't see anyone walking around that appeared to be a prostitute; every woman she saw outside was well-dressed, accompanied by some manner of gentleman or followed by nursemaids pushing baby carriages.

As they continued, the coach rode past at least three banks and a half dozen flower stalls, all of which had been freshly painted. They were clearly going through the nice end of town, she thought, and perhaps the buildings on the other side of the town were where they were hiding the scenes of poverty she had read about in books. Her father had told her about similar things after coming back from trips to Atlanta, and she figured that any large city would have its share of troubles.

Mary Ellen and her family had been wealthy before the war, but her father's tobacco plantation was one of many in northern Georgia that hadn't been able to sustain itself any longer after it was over. A large number of their slaves had been hired on to work the farm, but several were laid off after the first few months, including most of the domestic servants. Mary Ellen didn't mind having to cook her own meals, clean the house, plant crops, or dress herself, but it wasn't a lifestyle her mother could easily transition to. Being back in England with the wealth of her own family meant her mother could have the life of affluence she was used to. Mary Ellen thought of how much her father would have disapproved of "running home to Daddy" and not sticking it out at the farm. Being old enough to marry, she would have had her pick of young men back home—had there been many left alive who hadn't already married into the still thriving cotton plantation families.

Once at the train station, Edmund walked them to the train cars and helped them to their cabin. He told them the name of the coachman that would be waiting for them at the station and waved them goodbye as the train rolled away. Tucker and Robert fell sleep only a few minutes into the train ride, while Mary Ellen's mother sat quietly looking out the window at the countryside. Mary Ellen took out a pencil and a small notebook stuffed with blank postcards to write to Violet back home. She went on about the long boat ride and how vast the ocean was compared to the lake where they used to play. Violet was her previous maid whom Mary Ellen had secured a job for at a friend's plantation before they left. Her mother, claiming it would be inappropriate for her to have a black maid in

England, promised to get her a new one when they arrived.

"If I find they've been beating you," Mary Ellen wrote, "I'll send Tucker and Robert to burn the rest of her daddy's cotton down." The boys had accidentally set fire to a bale of hay there a couple years before, which resulted in the two of them having to help harvest more as punishment. Mary Ellen continued on about the coffee in the restaurant and how she would send her some as soon as she could.

Placing the notebook back into her dress pocket, she pulled out the small corncob pipe her father had given her. She had used it to test their tobacco crops back home, like her father had done. Her mother thought that, while it smelled nice, it tasted of burning shoe leather and disapproved of it in general. Mary Ellen had taken care to clean it before leaving, but some of the ashes still remained in the bowl. She rubbed the ashes between her fingers and put the pipe away just before the train pulled into the small station. Sure enough, there was the young coachman with a chalkboard sign that had "Murphy" scrawled crudely across it.

Mary Ellen couldn't help but notice how much nicer her grandfather's coach was than the hired one in town. It was clearly older than the other coach, yet great care had been taken to keep it looking brand new and clean. Perhaps the upholstery was newer, or it had been recently painted. She expected at any moment to see the level of wealth drop dramatically as they ventured out into the countryside, but instead the well-kept homes seemed to become more opulent.

For the first time in her life, Mary Ellen felt out of place.

The ride in the coach was much smoother than in town, even on the rough dirt roads leading to the estate from the small village station. The house at Redbriar had been run by her grandfather's side of the family for generations, and upon their arrival, Mary Ellen and her family were greeted by the staff, who quickly unloaded the coach, bringing their things upstairs.

The butler greeted her mother. "Lady Murphy, I am Mr. Taylor. You may remember my father."

She looked up at him in delight. "Oh, little Jack Taylor! The last time I saw you, you were no taller than this one here," she said, placing her hands on Tucker's shoulders. "How is your father?"

Mr. Taylor smiled. "He is doing well, Lady Murphy. Lord Hadaly set him up with a cottage on the estate."

"Good, he deserves it after having to put up with us for all these years." She smiled, leading the boys into the house while Mr. Taylor held the doors open. Mary Ellen walked in behind them and marveled at the exquisite details adorning the interior: Paintings on the wall that were no less than two hundred years old. Bright yellow-gold paint in every room, accented with crisp, white decorative molding. Stuffed birds in display cases, and various shields and swords mounted above reach. The entry hall floors were made of polished stone and covered in delicate carpets newly arrived from India. Furniture wrapped in fine silk upholstery, warm woods, and an unholy number of bookshelves—their Georgia plantation house was nothing like this. Sure, they had fine furniture and ornamental woodwork, but this was another world in comparison. Mary Ellen stood in awe of the grand staircases that split into two smaller sets of stairs that met at the very top of the third floor, all with ornate iron balusters. No piece of wood or metal in the house was left without embellishment. She now felt more out of place than ever.

Two nearly identical footmen walked up to them, both with light blue eyes and the same thin, bony faces. Their hair was slicked back in the exact same way, as though a mirror had been placed between them.

"Lady Murphy, Baron Hadaly is waiting in the study. Please follow me," one of them said.

The other looked at Mary Ellen and her brothers. "Miss Murphy, young masters, please follow me to your rooms." They even had the same voice, Mary Ellen thought.

Mary Ellen followed the footman up the first large set of stairs, which split into the two wings of the house. They went right and then up another set to a third floor. A long corridor dotted with doorways to various rooms seemed to go on forever. Several doors down they could see a group of young ladies in fresh white aprons standing at attention. The footman introduced two of the women as nurses who would be taking care of the boys, and another Mary Ellen assumed was going to be her new lady's maid. Between all of them was a much older, boney woman, with silver streaked temples, drawn cheeks, and her hair pulled up in a bun. She wore a chain from her pockets that clearly displayed the keys of the house and another chain that met to a pocket watch.

"Good evening my lady, my name is Mrs. Parker. I'm the housekeeper here at Redbriar. Should you require anything, please let Mrs. Harrison know and we will do our best to accommodate. I'm sure this is all very different from what you grew up with, so please do not hesitate to ask any questions."

Mary Ellen thanked her. "I'm sure we will get on just fine. But, might I ask when supper is?"

Mrs. Parker pulled out her silver pocket watch, giving it a quick glance. "Ah, If I don't get downstairs soon it will be after dark! Dinner is at seven. Mrs. Harrison will help you dress." She clapped her hands together. "If you will excuse us, my lady," she said, following the footman back down the hall.

"Come young masters, we need to get you cleaned up for dinner," one nursemaid said happily. The two nursemaids escorted Tucker and Robert to their room a few doors down. The boys cheered, having not eaten much at the cafe. The older maid shushed them, warning that they couldn't disturb everyone downstairs.

Mary Ellen turned to greet her new lady's maid, who was now holding the bedroom door open. "You too, my lady. You don't want to wash up with cold water." Mrs. Harrison closed the door behind them. The room was larger than the one she had back home and nearly as ornate as the downstairs parlor. It had two fireplaces, a bed, a desk with paper and pen, a washing basin, mirror and makeup table. Mrs.

Harrison quickly opened the steamer cases and began loading the contents into one of the three wardrobes. "Wash up, my lady, while I get these things unpacked."

Mary Ellen walked over to the wash basin, which still had somewhat warm water in it, and removed the dirty gloves she had been wearing all day. She washed her face quickly and began taking off her coat and placing it on the chair nearby. All she wanted to do was leap onto the bed and collapse for a few hours. Instead, she looked out the window at the vast countryside. There was nothing beyond the house other than rolling hills and trees. Mrs. Harrison pulled out a fresh dress and stockings, placing them on the bed.

"Mrs. Harrison?"

"Yes, my lady?"

"Where are all the animals?"

"Animals?"

"Yes, the cows and pigs and all."

Mrs. Harrison thought for a moment. "There is a stable on the other side of the house. The farms are all on the outside of the grounds. I'm afraid you aren't the only one who is new here."

The vastness of Redbriar in relation to what she had at home became apparent to Mary Ellen. "Ah, I see. This place is so much bigger than I'm used to, I guess."

"Oh yes, my lady, this estate is the biggest I've worked on," Mrs. Harrison said, walking over to Mary Ellen to start unbuttoning the back of her outer dress. "Most houses don't have near the staff of Redbriar."

Mrs. Harrison paused. "You had maids and all back home, I'm sure."

"My brothers and I shared a maid," Mary Ellen said. "Her name was Violet. Her momma named her that because of her eyes."

Mrs. Harrison perked up. "She had violet eyes?"

"Yes, but…" Mary Ellen said, not wanting to bring up any more visions of home. "If I could ask you a simple thing, Mrs. Harrison. I know you have rules and all for addressing me around the rest of the staff, but I'll go right out my mind if you keep calling me 'my lady' when they ain't around."

Mrs. Harrison finished unbuttoning the long line of fasteners and laces on the dress and pulled it up quickly, swapping it out for the new one. "And what would you prefer?"

Mary Ellen shuffled into the new dress, holding her arms out as Mrs. Harrison began connecting the back. "Miss, or Miss Mary Ellen is fine," she said. "And what's your name?"

"It's Margaret, Miss."

Once dressed and her hair put back in place, they walked downstairs to the dining room. Toby, one of the matching footmen, greeted them at the door and showed Mary Ellen and her brothers where they were to sit for dinner. Margaret and the nursemaids went on downstairs to the servant's area after getting the boys situated, since the boys were not used to such formal meals. Soon, their mother joined them, followed by an ancient man with wild, white hair. Mary Ellen had never met her grandfather, but when he looked at her, she saw her older brother in his eyes. It was as though

Jackson had never gone to war but traveled forward in time just to sit down and have dinner with them. That was, until he spoke. Baron Hadaly took one look at the silverware by his plate, examined it and pushed one of the forks forward so slightly it didn't appear to move at all. "Toby," he said in a guttural rumble. "Are we running a charity luncheon out on the greens?" Toby stood by him, slowly filling his master's glass with a golden sherry.

"No, Baron Hadaly."

"Standards, Toby, standards," he quipped.

"Yes, Baron Hadaly."

"Don't be so cruel, Papa," her mother said, taking a sip of her wine.

"Rosalind, my dear, you have no place telling me about cruelly treating staff." He motioned for the other matching footman to come to him. "William, my boy, tell my daughter how much we pay you per year." William leaned to her mother and quietly told her the sum. Baron Hadaly pointed his finger at her. "Now, I want the boys to hear this, because it is of the utmost importance. We pay our staff a *living* wage here. Twenty percent more than the going rates in the city."

"I don't think this is appropriate conversation for dinner, Papa. The war is over anyhow, we freed our workers over two years ago. We haven't *owned* anyone since."

"And never will again, God willing."

Mary Ellen sat in silence, her face blushing from embarrassment as she sipped her soup.

"I expect the lot of you to treat my staff as fellow human beings. It takes a small army to keep this house running, and I will not have any of you mistreating them."

"Of course, Papa. We wouldn't dream of ruining the reputation of Redbriar."

Mary Ellen looked over at her mother, now curious as to what story was behind the comment.

"Alright, alright. Enough," he said, conceding to eat his soup quietly for a few moments. "So, Mary Ellen, how old are you now?"

"Seventeen," she answered.

He nearly dropped his spoon. "And not yet engaged? Come now, Rosalind, we have to get this girl out in society as quickly as possible."

"War makes it difficult to shop for potential husbands, Papa," her mother said.

"Well my dear," he said, looking at Mary Ellen through his tiny round glasses. "There are several proper families with eligible men fit to take the reins of this noble house. I'll have Mrs. Parker and your mother make this their top priority."

Mary Ellen was confused. She had assumed her uncle Edmund would be taking over the estate. Now, she had an idea as to what her mother was alluding to. Had he gone and married a common woman in the city? She was sure Margaret would know and made a note to ask her as soon as she got back to her room.

"I can hardly contain my excitement, Baron Hadaly," Mary Ellen said, as one of the footmen took her empty soup bowl from the table.

"Now, now, I'm Grandpa to you, young lady. You're a Hadaly as much as you are a Murphy."

"Paw Paw Hadaly!" Tucker said in excitement.

"Yes, my boy?"

"Can we ride the horses tomorrow?!"

"You most certainly can, child. I'll have Taylor arrange it in the morning," he said, taking a sip of his sherry. "Do you know how to ride a pony?"

Both boys nodded in unison, their mouths full of roast pheasant.

Rosalind gave her father a look, "They've never ridden a horse in their lives, Papa."

He laughed. "Oh, it's nice to have a full set of Hadalys at the table again."

After dinner, Margaret met back up with Mary Ellen to get her ready for bed. "Miss Margaret, is it alright if we take a little walk outside? I've been sitting in chairs all day."

"Of course lady—Miss Mary Ellen," she said, and rushed into the room to grab their coats. As they walked around the grounds of the estate, they watched the sun set further and further into the trees in the distance. Mary Ellen didn't speak the entire trip, until they reached the edge of the large garden. It was filled with a multitude of plants and trees, walking paths, and six fully working fountains. She wondered what it would look like when spring arrived and all the flowers were in bloom.

"It's getting dark, Miss Mary Ellen. We should head back soon," Margaret said, watching one of the boys on staff climbing up the newly installed, gas lamp post and lighting it with a stick. Mary Ellen sighed and nodded. The wind was beginning to bite through her jacket, and her gloves were just a little too thin for the climate. Her clothes were warm enough for Georgia autumns but not so much here. Margaret spoke up again just before they reached the midpoint of the garden walls.

"We can get you some warmer dresses made this week. I noticed the ones you brought were in need of mending."

Mary Ellen nodded.

"Are you alright, Miss Mary Ellen?"

She stopped walking and looked at Margaret. "I guess not." She didn't know that her thin, old ratted dresses were her nicest ones she had, and they were nearly two years old. Her mother instructed her on how things worked in England and not mention to anyone, including her new maid, what level of poverty they had fallen into after the war.

"You just need to sleep, is all. You'll feel better in the morning, I'm sure of it."

The girls walked back to the house and up the stairs to the bedroom where Mary Ellen was quickly set up for bed. She wasn't used to such nice and clean bedding. Before they left the house, they had sold much of their furniture, and at one point ended up sharing the last bed with her brothers and Violet while her mother slept on the last remaining sofa. On the long boat ride over, they couldn't afford upscale rooms, or even standard ones, and had to spend ten days on hard cots in third class.

"If you need anything Miss, I'll be right next door."

Mary Ellen mumbled something in agreement into the pillow before rapidly falling asleep.

The next morning, Margaret was up early and lighting one of the fireplaces. The sound of the fire crackling woke her suddenly, the sun not quite up. Mary Ellen shot up, not sure where she was.

"I'm sorry Miss, didn't mean to wake you," Margaret whispered, "Go back to sleep."

"What time is it?"

"Nearly six a.m."

"Why?"

"Why is it six a.m.?"

"I don't know," Mary Ellen answered, before collapsing back into bed.

"Get some rest. I'll wake you when breakfast is ready."

Margaret went back to her room and quietly worked on cleaning Mary Ellen's shoes, which were clearly over worn and needed severe repair. She worked for a while before hearing Mary Ellen get out of bed in the next room to use the water closet, followed by the sound of clothes moving around, then the unmistakable opening of the door. She bolted up from her chair to meet Mary Ellen in the hallway. "What on earth are you doing, Miss Mary Ellen?!" she shouted in a whisper.

"I'm going downstairs to get a coffee," Mary Ellen whispered back.

"You can't go down to the kitchen while the staff is cooking breakfast! I'll go get you a coffee. Get back in the room right now before someone sees you!"

It then dawned on Mary Ellen that Margaret could get in trouble if the rules weren't followed and the blame was placed on her lack of instruction. "Sorry. I'll go hide in there 'till you get back."

Several minutes later, Margaret returned with a silver tray holding a pot of coffee, bread, jam, and a couple of hard-boiled eggs. "My previous mistress used to always take her food in her room, but I think you should go down later and eat a little something with the rest of the family. At least for the first few weeks. Not sure how you take your coffee, so I brought cream, sugar, and milk."

Mary Ellen was sitting at her drawing table, looking over the stationery and contemplating writing another letter. "I just take it black. Sorry, I'm still used to doing some things myself, you understand. This will all take some getting used to."

"Mrs. Parker doesn't directly oversee my work, but that doesn't mean I'm immune to her ability to replace me if she thinks I'm not doing my job."

"She runs this whole place like a hotel, huh?"

"I suppose so," Margaret said, filling the cup with light brown coffee. "My previous mistress rarely traveled, so I've only stayed in two or three hotels."

Mary Ellen took a sip of the coffee and winced. The kitchen had managed to make the coffee weak, scorched, and disgusting at the same time. "Well, I don't want the cook to get fired on account of me, but at some point today, we need to sit him down and show him how to make proper coffee."

"Or I can bring a pot up here and you can show me how to do it, then I can relay it to the chef. That way no toes are stepped on," Margaret said, pulling a small pad of paper from her apron. "I'll add it to the list. I have to turn it in to Mrs. Parker after luncheon so let me know before then and it will get put on order.

After breakfast I have to get your measurements, so we can get the fabric ordered in for your new dresses."

"Papa Hadaly isn't kidding about that society stuff, is he?"

"I should suspect not," Margaret said, opening the curtains to the room and letting the early morning light in. "With both your uncles out of the picture, you're left to secure this estate."

"What happened with my other uncle? I met one in London and he seemed to be doing well enough."

Margaret leaned in and whispered, "Well, I'm not supposed to say, Miss, but I figure you've a right to know given it's your family and all."

Mary Ellen listened intently, taking a large bite from one of the eggs.

Margaret shook her head.

"Sorry, my manners seem to have died with the Confederacy." Mary Ellen picked up the spoon and placed it back in the egg cup to finish.

"Right, so, your uncle in London works for a bank. He sends some of his earnings back to the estate now and then but nothing serious, but he's never married and is older than your mum."

"I get ya. What do you know about the other one?"

"Now, him everyone knows about because it made the papers, and gossip around here gets on like a house on fire. Don't worry, he didn't murder anyone or anything like that, but he got caught messing with the taxes for the estate. Stealing money from the tenants, telling 'em the taxes had gone up when they hadn't. When your grandfather found out, he called the constables on him, got put in jail for a year. His wife left 'em. She and the kids moved up to

Manchester. She remarried, so the kids don't have claim to the estate anymore."

"Huh, what did they do about the extra tax money?"

"Your grandfather went through every book and repaid each tenant personally."

"When was all this?"

"A year ago, I think. I hear he got out of jail and hopped a boat to New York or something. That's what Mr. Taylor says anyway."

Mary Ellen sat up from her chair, ran to the water closet, opened the lid and promptly vomited into the bowl.

"Miss Murphy are you alright?" Margaret shouted.

Mary Ellen continued for a few minutes, until the dry heaves kicked in. Margaret went to the tray of food to check the egg and toast before opening the coffee pot to find a single purple flower floating inside. She instantly ran over to the wall and rung the bell to Mrs. Parker's office, the maid's rooms, and the kitchen. "Keep trying to get it up, Miss!"

"Those sons of be—" she said, vomiting again.

Within a few minutes Mrs. Parker was at the door. "What seems to be the trouble?"

"Lady Murphy hasn't been here a whole day and one of your little devils downstairs tried to poison her already!" Margaret snapped, holding the small flower she fished out of the coffee pot.

Mrs. Parker's face went white. She rushed over to Mary Ellen, who was now throwing up blood-tinged bile. She called for one of the maids to run downstairs and fetch something from her room, handing her a single key from her chain. "You'll be alright, Lady Murphy, just keep bringing it up."

"I think that's all of it," Mary Ellen said, before coughing up more bile and chunks of soft-boiled egg.

"How much of the coffee did she drink?" Mrs. Parker asked in a fury.

Margaret looked over at the half empty cup. "Not much, she said it didn't taste good in the first place."

"And you brought it up to her?"

"Aye, Mrs. Parker, but I didn't see who set it up. I just placed it on the tray, I swear."

"Not a word of this leaves this room, do you understand me?"

"Aye, Mrs. Parker," Margaret answered. "I've got a pot of water in my room. Should we give her some?"

"Yes, hurry."

Margaret dashed across the room to her small chamber and came back with a pitcher of water she had planned to use for the wash basin. She poured some into a clean mug and handed it to Mrs. Parker.

"You sip it first," Mrs. Parker ordered. She knocked back the entire cup and refilled it. "Alright my lady, I need you to drink some of this."

Mary Ellen drank the water and promptly threw it up again.

By then, the maids returned with Mrs. Parker's key and a vial of black powder. "Quickly, quickly!" Mrs. Parker said to the girl, taking the vial and emptying a few dashes of it into the cup of water.

Mary Ellen drank from it and winced. "Sweet hell, what is this?!

"Don't you worry yourself about that, my lady, it will keep the stomach from bleeding." Mary Ellen launched a tirade of expletives as she choked down the gritty water.

"Now, now, do I need to get the soap as well, young lady?" Mrs. Parker said, helping her up on the chair again. Margaret brought over a large bucket, asking one of the maids to bring her two more. She quickly emptied the bowl from the water closet into the bucket, holding her breath to keep from gagging. Mrs. Parker pulled out her pocket watch and waited. A few minutes passed. Finally, she sent the rest of the maids off to do their chores and put a stop to breakfast being served until she could go back down to inspect it.

"Alright, it's been long enough now, I think. Let's get you back in bed," Mrs. Parker said as she and Margaret helped get Mary Ellen out of the chair. "Just keep her drinking the water, and let her vomit if she has to. I'll send for a doctor when I get downstairs." She then leaned over to Margaret and whispered, "She may start acting queer in a few hours, Just don't let her out of the bedroom, you understand?" Margaret nodded, knowing the effects of the little purple flower.

Downstairs, Mrs. Parker lined up her small army of servants in the kitchen hallway. In front of her was a plate of all the breakfast items intended to be served that morning. She took a fork and carefully sampled a bite of everything on the plate, watching the faces of the staff as she did so. "Now, as you all know, someone tried to poison Lady Murphy's daughter this morning." She took a bite of egg. "And you all should know that such a crime is not only cause for dismissal without references, but also completely against the law." A bite of sausage and toast followed. "I have the constable on his way as we speak, and if no one comes forward I may be forced to replace this entire staff as it stands." She picked up a teacup and brought it to her lips. The shaking of one of the kitchen boys caught her eye and she walked over to him with the cup. "Mr. Parson, it is awfully cold in this hallway. Would you care for a cup of tea?" she asked handing it to him.

He stammered, "N-no, mum. Mrs. Parker."

"And why not?"

"Cuz, it's got foxglove innit."

She stared him down so hard he thought her glasses were going to shatter. "Pray tell, why on God's heavenly earth does the Baron's breakfast tea have foxglove in it?"

"Cuz, his daughter's a bloody slaver!" he shouted and made a quick dash for the back door, only to be caught seconds later by one of the footmen. They struggled as the boy continued yelling. "She'll have the lot of you in chains!"

"I regret to inform everyone that Mr. Parson has been let go." Mrs. Parker said aloud. "And I'm afraid breakfast will be without tea this morning until every pot and kettle has been thoroughly scrubbed."

2

The English Drink Gin

Mary Ellen was awakened later that night by a freezing cold towel being placed on her forehead. She sat up slowly and tossed it to the floor. A wave of nausea forced her to lay back down on the bed. The room spun, and her vision distorted. She had been drunk before. Back home, she and Violet had split a half bottle of whiskey they found in her father's old bedroom, but this wasn't quite the same. Her muscles ached, as though she he had been laying out tobacco to dry during harvest season.

Margaret was in a chair nearby, mending one of her petticoats. "Now, now, Miss Mary Ellen, doctor says you need to take it easy for a day or so," she said, putting the petticoat on the chair and walking over to check her forehead. "But it looks like the fever is passed. Let me know when you get hungry, and I can go downstairs for some soup."

"What…happened?" Mary Ellen stuttered.

"One of the kitchen boys poisoned your coffee this morning when I wasn't looking," Margaret said. "But don't you worry Miss, Mrs. Parker had the constable come take him away this morning."

"What did Granddaddy say about it?"

Margaret looked at her, holding her cold hand. "That's the thing Miss, Mrs. Parker told the Baron what happened, but he told your mother that you had taken ill after the journey."

Mary Ellen nodded. "Good. She doesn't take things well."

"We had the doctor come and check on you as a 'precaution', and he said once the fever broke, you would be fine in a day or so."

"I don't remember."

"It's alright, Miss. If you're up for it, cook made you some soup earlier. I can run down and fetch it."

"And how do I know that's not poisoned too?"

"Oh Miss, the whole staff is on edge about it. They wouldn't dare. Mrs. Parker threatened to sack everyone downstairs without references if the food gives anyone so much as indigestion."

Mary Ellen sat up again, careful not to make herself too dizzy, and got down off the bed. She walked over to her leather notebook and pulled out a small iron key. "That bottom drawer of my case."

Margaret took the key from her and opened the locked section of the luggage. Inside was a leather pouch with something incredibly heavy inside.

"Bring it over here," Mary Ellen said, sitting down at her desk chair. Margaret did so and Mary Ellen opened the pouch, pulling out a wound-up cloth. She unraveled the floral sackcloth to display a shining brown handle, followed by the silver length of a Colt Navy Revolver.

"Don't worry," she said, checking the cylinder. "I'm out of cartridges."

"Why do you have that, Miss?"

"This was my daddy's service revolver. Momma tried to pawn it before we left, so I hid it," she said, wrapping the gun back in its pretty floral cloth. "You can spread whatever rumors you want to the kitchen boys downstairs about it though. Let them know there are worse things to deal with than Mrs. Parker," she said, putting the gun in one of the drawers of her writing desk. "I think I'd like that soup now though."

Mary Ellen walked over to the door and gently eased it open just enough to see when Margaret descended the stairs. The moment she was out of sight, she walked as quickly as her still numb legs would let her over to her trunk and checked the unlocked drawer. She pulled out four small boxes that were tucked away in the back, along with another, much older leather-bound notebook and hid them in her writing desk. Her joints ached as she sat down at the desk again, pulling one of her small blankets around her shoulders. Even with the fireplace burning, the area by the window in the evening was extraordinary cold. It reminded her of standing by the fire in winter back home, when the side closest to the fire scorched and the other side froze.

She opened the old leather notebook and glanced through the first few pages. It was the diary she kept back home before the war. She had written about how much she hated her French lessons one day. Another page recalled how handsome a friend's older brother looked at a party. She skipped ahead to when her father left to join the war and how much her mother protested it, writing that he was the only thing she really loved about living in Georgia. A few pages later covered her upset at the fact that her older brother was joining her father after reading about the victories in the paper. She skipped through several more pages to the days when her mother was trying to run the plantation, getting into arguments with the foreman almost daily about the slaves working conditions. She pulled a small yellowed newspaper clipping from one page, an advertisement for tobacco from the North that advertised below the price they were selling it at in bulk. Several more pages forward, she glanced through the troubled times of the failing plantation, having to work in the fields herself, being taught how to cook her own meals, up to the news that her father and brother would not be returning home. Blank pages filled the remainder of the notebook. Closing it, she unconsciously picked up her pipe and bit down on the mouthpiece.

Margaret returned armed with a large tray of food. She placed it down on the small table near the bed as she had done before. "Alright Miss, I've got a lamb stew, bread, and some jam."

"No coffee this time?"

"I didn't think you'd be up for it, Miss. Come now over here and eat by the fire."

Mary Ellen sat down on the stuffed chair by the fireplace and looked over the food.

Margaret put her hands on her hips in frustration. "Alright," she said, taking a bit of the bread, dipping it into the soup and eating it herself.

Mary Ellen paused, waiting for her to swallow the food. Margaret then poured a cup of tea and took a sip to wash down the bread that didn't' quite make it down to her stomach. "See, Miss, I promise you, nothing...wrong...with..." She grabbed at her throat, poorly pretending to gasp for air before extravagantly falling to the floor.

Mary Ellen smiled. "Alright, I get ya," she said, pouring her own cup of tea and taking a sip. Her first reaction was to the fact that it was cold, her second was to the fact that it was beer.

"What in the..."

"Mrs. Parker has rules about alcohol being sent upstairs. She's somewhat of a teetotaler—keeps it all under lock and key until meals are served. We get ale at dinner and I filled a teapot when nobody was looking. Thought you might need it."

"Bless your heart," she said, slathering a piece of bread with jam. "And I mean that in a good way."

Margaret reached over to the mantle of the fireplace and placed two vials on the tray. "Here, doctor says you needed to take a few drops of these after you've eaten."

Mary Ellen looked at the bottles as she ate. "What in the sweet hell is chlorodyne?" she asked, the three teacups of beer on an empty stomach enhancing her vocabulary.

Margaret shrugged, "He said it was to help with any aches you might have afterwards. Said you can't have it until you've eaten though."

"Did y'all not eat supper yet?" she said, now eating the soup. "What time is it anyway?"

"Nearly eleven, Miss."

"At night?!"

"Yes, Miss, and I still need to take your tray downstairs."

"You need to go in bed in yer little room back in there, 'n get some sleep! Them's too long of hours!" Mary Ellen stammered, slamming her spoon on the table. "You can't run a house like this, this is… is how accidents happen and folks get cut, lack of sleep 'n all. D'you know how hard it is to get bloodstains off tobacco?" She continued on, standing up from her chair and trying to walk Margaret to her room. "You, you, need to sleep. I've been asleep all damn day. You need to sleep."

Margaret walked along, holding Mary Ellen up as they went. "We're not on a farm Miss, and Mrs. Parker will wonder where the dinner tray has gone."

"Mrs. Parker can shove that tray up her skirts. You. Go. To. Sleep." Mary Ellen said, closing the door to the room the second Margaret passed through the doorway. "And I don't want to see you come through this door until eight o'clock!"

"But, Miss, I have duties."

"Eight. O. Clock-uh."

The next morning Mary Ellen awoke to see the tray removed and the fire re-lit.

"Damnit, Margaret I said not to get up till after eight."

"It's nine thirty, Mary Ellen," her mother said from her perch on the stuffed chair.

"Momma!"

"I see you are feeling better, dear, but I can't present you to society if you are going to talk like a field hand."

"Yes ma'am," she said. Getting up from the bed, she noticed her mother was fully dressed—hat, gloves, everything. "Are you going somewhere?"

"I came up here to tell you I'm going back to London for a week or so. I know we just arrived here, but I have important business to handle to get you ready for the season in time. You would already be out in society in Atlanta if it weren't for the war, but we must make do with the time we have."

"Shouldn't I go with you then?"

Her mother shook her head. "No, Mrs. Harrison needs you here to make your dresses and to take your measurements. I want you to keep an eye on your brothers while I'm gone. Spend some time with your grandfather and get to know the house. He can fill you in on the history."

"Yes ma'am" Mary Ellen said, walking over to kiss her mother goodbye.

"Goodbye, dear."

Margaret soon arrived and helped Mary Ellen clean up and get dressed. She brought up a tray of coffee, kippers wrapped in pastry, and a poached egg along with some bread and jam. Mary Ellen ate quickly and let Margaret get to work on taking her measurements for the new clothes she most desperately needed. Just looking at her current clothes, Margaret could tell she had outgrown them at least a year ago, and wasn't about to let her mistress be seen outside in frayed cotton dresses.

"Where did you find these gloves?" Mary Ellen asked.

"Oh, I mended them yesterday, Miss."

"But they look new!"

"Nothing a good brushing can't do," she said, bringing her a pair of shoes. Mary Ellen was used to cleaning and mending her own clothes, but Margaret's skill was at a professional level.

"No, you've let out the knuckles too. Do all ladies maids do this?"

Margaret gave her a quiet look. "I used to be a seamstress in Ireland before working in houses. Married an Englishman at sixteen who worked in a dress shop. It— well, caught fire." She stopped for a moment to keep her voice from shaking. "Nothing for me back in Ireland and the other shops won't hire me. Working in houses at least I can still sew."

"I'm so sorry, Margaret."

"Don't worry none about me, Miss," she said taking a measuring tape to Mary Ellen's shoulders. "It's been nearly four years now. Time to move on, I suppose. Can't hide in Balmoral forever."

"What?" Mary Ellen asked, not being up to date on English news.

"Oh nothing, Miss. You're done," Margaret said, putting the tape around her neck and scribbling down the numbers on a pad of paper. "You're supposed to go downstairs to see your grandfather before luncheon, so you best head that way."

Mary Ellen went downstairs and let Margaret get to work. She walked through the long corridors, taking in the artwork and relics placed along the walls. Outside a door stood her grandfather's valet, he greeted her and let her into the study that her grandfather was working in.

"Mary Ellen, my dear! Come sit over here," he cheered, pulling out a plum upholstered wooden chair. "Would you care for some tea?"

She declined, explaining that she had just eaten a late breakfast.

"Well, I'm glad to see you're doing well enough to come down." He went on for over an hour, explaining his position as a Baron and what that means to her and the schedule for coming out in society, which would correspond with his requirements in the House of Lords during the parliamentary season. While Redbriar was their estate, the family owned several houses scattered around the Empire. Their London home, the one Uncle Edmund was currently residing in, would be where they would stay during the season. There a was a hunting cottage up in the highlands where he used to take his sons when they were younger. He also mentioned a handful of hotel residencies in notable continental cities such as Paris, St. Petersburg, and Cairo. There was even a house in New York that was given to his oldest son after his excommunication from the family. Baron Hadaly explained that he would never visit the States again because of his son.

"When I'm gone, Mary Ellen, your mother is to take over as Baroness of Redbriar." Mary Ellen was certain that her uncle was next in line for the peerage.

"But, grandfather, what about—"

He quickly cut her off. "Your uncle Edmund, bless him, is an excellent businessman. Half the banks in London run under him, however, he wants nothing to do with the title that afforded him the luxury of his profession. Which leaves it to your mother."

"What if she hadn't come home?"

"That is something we need to discuss, my dear. My brother's sons were poised to take over the estate when I pass. But now, with your mother back, they are no longer in the running. Your cousins, which you will meet in society when you go to London, may not be so keen to meet with you. They may even be hostile to your presence. One would expect them to behave kindly to you given their breeding, however I must warn you, should they send invitations or call, be cautious of them. Hopefully my assumptions are wrong, and they will do everything in their power to befriend you." He stood up and looked out the window of the study. "Even then, one should keep an eye on their intentions."

Mary Ellen agreed, thanking her grandfather for the warning. She was used to the expectations of making calls and hosting parties, as her mother had before the war. "Now your mother is in London, securing a list of trustworthy acquaintances as well as potential husbands. I only ask that you not only look for a successful man but look into how he became successful. Some of the richest men in London are absolute tyrants; their fathers were tyrants as grandfathers before. If he runs a mill or factory, visit the conditions of it—it will reflect on how he will surely treat you. Industrialization is changing the world Mary Ellen, and good breeding won't be enough to keep an estate running in the next fifty years. One must be proactive these days." He was interrupted by a loud knocking on the door. "Come in!"

"Lord Hadaly, your appointment is here."

"Thank you, Mr. Taylor," he said and turned to his granddaughter, "Excuse me, Mary Ellen, I'm afraid our chat must come to an end. Feel free to explore the grounds until luncheon."

Mary Ellen spent the rest of the morning strolling through the long hallways and rooms. She found at least three libraries, a smoking room that clearly hadn't been smoked in for ages, a small ballroom that could host a good number of guests for a large party, and a host of locked guest rooms only to be bothered when they were needed. She then made her way down to where the servants worked, as she wanted to see the kitchen. A few scullery maids skittered past as she walked through the hallway, the staff were making final preparations for luncheon and were very busy. Mrs. Parker and Margaret caught her just as she was about to reach the kitchen.

"Lady Murphy, I hope there is nothing wrong."

"No, Mrs. Parker. I was simply touring the house and wanted to see the kitchen."

"Poor Margaret has been looking all over for you. I can show you the kitchens after service is over. We can't be in the way of the cook in the middle of service. Now, go upstairs and get ready for luncheon."

"Of course, Mrs. Parker. Oh," she said, pulling a small note of paper from her pocket. "I've also written that list you requested."

"Thank you, now out of here the both of you. This battlefield is no place for a lady!"

After luncheon, Mary Ellen had to try on the linen templates that Margaret stitched together earlier in the day. Of course, they fit perfectly. Margaret was used to sewing up to five full dresses a week, for her, three templates was nothing.

While the week went on, Mary Ellen spent her days walking around the grounds, finally visiting the kitchen and seeing how much work it took to keep an estate of Redbriar's size running. She met with the stableman, the groundskeepers, various service boys and cleaning maids, making a note to remember their names for the next time she met them. Margaret had finished the dresses in time for Mary Ellen's mother's arrival back to the estate. Her mother met with her upstairs after dinner.

"These are beautiful, Margaret. You're an exceptional seamstress. You make the London shop dresses look like prison rags." Her mother gushed over the near perfect seams around the sleeves as Mary Ellen modeled them for her in her room. Not only did she bring over more fabric for dresses but several new pairs of kidskin gloves, as well as new shoes. She also brought the boys some of the new, ready-made knickerbockers and a few suits. Mary Ellen loved the new gloves; she hadn't worn new ones in years. Her mother brought out a large file filled with pages, along with a box of custom printed stationery with Mary Ellen's name.

"Here is a list of suitable acquaintances, notable people about town, and those of potential marriage material. I want you to look over it and start writing cards to them. In two months, you're going with me to London to start making calls before the season starts.

We need everyone to know who you are before you arrive." Mary Ellen was weary of the whole situation, having been working a tobacco field only a month ago, she was now preparing herself to mingle with not just the leading nobility of England, but a fleeting audience with Queen Victoria herself.

"Did you go through all of this too, Momma?"

"Yes, dear, and believe me, we have much work to do. You can get away with murder in America, but one social blunder here will ruin your chances for a husband forever." She looked over at the small table in Mary Ellen's room. "I see you've outfitted yourself with a little bar." She pointed out the bottle of bourbon and small glasses.

"Don't worry, Momma, it's just to calm the nerves."

Her mother gave her a knowing look. "The English drink gin."

3

The London House

Two months of letter writing and clothes fittings were winding up to the trip to London. Mary Ellen was excited to be going to the big city again, having grown tired of being locked away in the estate house. She often took long walks around the estate and would have gotten herself lost if Margaret wasn't keeping an eye on her.

Margaret had sewn almost a dozen dresses, all with matching hats. Mary Ellen's favorite was a dark blue wool dress that was meant for daily wear. She liked it because it was the warmest of them all. Still not quite acclimated to the drastic change in climate, she often felt incredibly cold in the drafty halls of the estate. Every night Margaret would put enough coals on the fire to ensure it stayed somewhat lit, knowing Mary Ellen would get up if she was too cold and feed the fire herself in the middle of the night.

The day had finally come to load up the family coach and make their way to the village train station outside the estate. Her brothers were upset at having to stay at Redbriar without their sister or mother, but Baron Hadaly promised to take them to the village for a ride and some candy while they were gone. Their mother reminded them that they would soon be going off to school and would need to get used to living away from her.

On the way to the train station, the inside of the coach was freezing, though the train cars after that were even colder. Mary Ellen bundled up and wished that her mother would have spent less on their private train cabin so they could be in one of the cars with more bodies to keep it warm. It wasn't until they reached the London house that she could finally shrug off the cold.

Her uncle was there to greet them at the door, his footmen guiding her and Margaret up to their rooms while her mother stayed downstairs to chat. The London house was a reasonably-sized town-home. While still grand and well decorated, the scale of it was more down to earth. It had only one staircase and two floors. No huge wings or land surrounded it, and the walls of the house melted into the walls of its neighbor, creating a sandwich of homes that could only be separated by the front doorway and the change of color on the outside. She looked out her bedroom window in awe of the city street below, watching people walk down the sidewalk on the other side of the gated iron wall. It reminded her of her old house in Georgia—cozy and welcoming, not cold and empty like Redbriar. The girls unloaded her things and set out clothes for dinner. Her uncle did not keep a cook, having his staff bring in their own lunch and go out to the street stalls for breakfast and dinner. Of course, he paid them a little extra to do this, but it saved him the cost of keeping a chef full time as he was always at the office and grabbed his own meals from the street vendors or pubs and supper clubs with co-workers.

The London house only required a butler, two footmen and his own valet. The footmen doubled as cleaning maids and the butler acted as housekeeper given the minimal effort needed to keep the house in order. He rarely brought guests over to visit, save for special occasions. It was apparent the reason her uncle was so good at banking was that he was impeccably efficient and didn't spend as lavishly as his father's estate afforded him.

Mary Ellen grew concerned by this. "I hope they don't expect you to go scrubbing walls too," she said to Margaret. "Ain't right to leave you here alone with all grown men servants in the house. If we go somewhere, I'll insist you come along."

Margaret laughed and agreed anyway. "Which of these new kids do you want out for dinner, Miss?" she asked sorting through a box filled with gloves.

"Do I really have to wear gloves to dinner, here? We're not at the Lord's-Sir-Majesty's castle. Uncle Edmund has food brought in as it is. Couldn't imagine eating barbeque in gloves back home."

"Maybe you can use the kitchen while we're here and cook some," Margaret said, pulling out a silver-grey pair.

"Hah, you gotta cook barbeque outside. But that doesn't mean I can't go cook some biscuits and gravy in the morning. Given there's some flour down there," she said, scribbling something in her journal.

"You're havin' a laugh, Miss. Gravy with biscuits. You Yanks have the strangest—"

Mary Ellen appeared before her suddenly, hitting Margaret across the face with her notebook. The slap of the leather echoed through the room. Margaret stumbled back in shock more than pain.

"Yankees killed my daddy. Yankees killed my brother. I had to abandon everyone I loved back home because of Yankees. Never call me that word again, Mrs. Harrison."

"Forgive me my lady, I didn't know the difference."

"You will not call me my lady! If you can't remember that, I can find someone who can."

Margaret crossed her arms in anger. "Come now, Miss. If you're gonna sack me for that I'll speak my piece first."

"Speak it," Mary Ellen demanded.

"You got handed a shite hand, yeah, but look where you are now!" Margaret stood facing her, just slightly taller. "You stand to become a Baroness, more wealth than most people can ever imagine in their lives. Now, I'm sorry about your family but that's war, Mary Ellen, a war that's given your old 'workers' a chance at a proper lot in life. You might be used to beating yer old maid with books, but I'm not about to put up with it. You know how many others were in line for this job? Two! No decent folk want to work for slave owners." Margaret watched the tears run down Mary Ellen's stone angry face.

Mary Ellen collapsed in the chair beside the bed, weeping. "I never beat her," she choked.

"Oh, so the slave-driver spares the rod for the ones she likes, eh?"

"She was my sister."

Margaret froze. "What?"

Mary Ellen nodded. "Half-sister."

Margaret stood back in shock. "What? Why would your mother leave one of her children behind? Much less force them into servitude?"

"She was my father's. I didn't know until I was older. When we left, she asked to stay with her mother, and Momma didn't object to it." Mary Ellen broke down in tears.

Margaret instinctively rushed to console her. "That's why she had violet eyes, then?" she asked, wiping Mary Ellen's face with a handkerchief.

She nodded. "I'm sorry I got upset. I shouldn't have hit you." Mary Ellen shot up from the chair, "You're not going to leave, are you?"

Margaret laughed. "Of course not, Miss. If I quit over every rotten little girl that hit me in the face with a book, I'd be out on the street."

"I promise it won't happen again Margaret."

"If I had a shilling for every time I heard that, Miss, I'd have a year's wages."

Mary Ellen finished getting ready and headed down to the dining room at the time requested by her uncle, which was a strict 7:15 p.m. Food was delivered to the house by different local restaurants. All of her uncle's favorites, of course. He had hundreds of friends in town, including every business owner he had made loans for at amazing rates. It was no wonder he stayed unmarried. If he were to settle down with a wife, he wouldn't have time to go out to parties and gentlemen's clubs for dinner every other day. Dinner was a quiet affair of the freshest oysters. The dining room was much smaller than Redbriar's but still large enough for a dozen people to eat in. It was cozy and butted up to the kitchen, which could be seen through a door at the other end. Mary Ellen waved when she saw Margaret eating her dinner in the kitchen along with the rest of the staff. She waved back, holding up what appeared to be the same oysters that she and her family were eating.

The second course was roast pork and potatoes. After the meal was over, her uncle got up from the table and asked everyone to meet him outside by the doorway.

"And bring your dish and spoon."

They walked out to the front entry garden where there was a young man with his penny ice cream cart. Mary Ellen and her mother got their scoops first, followed by Margaret and the rest of the staff. Her uncle was last, and he tipped the boy after paying for the ice creams. Everyone sat outside on the wooden benches, having their dessert in the chilly November air, followed by coffee and tea inside before bed. Mary Ellen could see why her uncle would be so care-free with social expectations. Having grown up at the well-oiled machine that was Redbriar, who wouldn't forgo all convention and have fun with their lives if they could?

The next few weeks went by quickly, with many appointments and lessons. When she wasn't studying which fork to use, she had to brush up on current events and make at least two calls every afternoon. She, her mother, and Margaret would all get a cab and go down to some other well-to-do house for a visit after lunch. Each house was written to, and the following day they would drive over for a fifteen to twenty-minute meetup.

Mary Ellen had picked up a new notebook just to jot down who it was she was meeting and what they looked like, as well as the address and what they talked about during the call. Most of it was her mother talking, as she knew the lady of the house from childhood and the whole purpose of the visit was to introduce Mary Ellen to her old friends in person. Margaret always stayed behind in the cab if it was raining or wandered around a stall or shop nearby if it was clear.

The perks of visiting London were that one could buy anything in the streets. She bought some candy one day, new thread on another, needles, spare boning, and some nice ribbons as well. By the end of the week, she had done all the odd shopping she would have normally had put an order in for back at Redbriar. One particularly cold afternoon, there was a series of book vendors along the street where they had parked. Margaret went over to find herself something fresh to read when she saw a tobacconist stall nearby. She smelled a few jars of them and bought sixpence worth of one she felt was alright.

Once back at the London house, Mary Ellen went upstairs to go over her notes and warm up by the fireplace. "How did today's go?" Margaret asked, knitting something with her new fabrics.

"I can't tell if we're making a good impression or not with some of these folks," Mary Ellen said, scribbling down information beside one of the names. "Lady Carlisle didn't seem one bit interested in me, and just chatted away with Momma about something they did as kids. It's how they all go."

"She has an eligible son, then?"

"Yeah, but I didn't catch his age. Can't meet them in person until the season starts, since they are all away at university or working with their fathers. We're getting approval from 'dearest mother' first."

"Any luck yet?"

"I've got two cards this week from some that were too busy to meet, nothing from the others yet. I'm not too worried about it. Would you send a note to a childhood friend's daughter you just met for a quarter hour?"

"You'll be fine, Miss. We'll get you ready for the season and you'll have cards coming in like overdue bills."

"I hope so. Momma's running herself ragged trying to get me out there early. But she seems to know what she is doing." Mary Ellen put her notes down and collapsed into her desk chair. "You get more ribbons today?"

Margaret nodded. "I may send a boy out to get more of this blue ribbon," she said holding it up. "I think it goes good with your blonde hair."

"Just no green," Mary Ellen said. "I keep seeing women out with this bright green ribbon. It's hideous."

"Oh wait, I did get you something, Miss," Margaret said, pulling the cloth pouch from her coat pocket. "I didn't know what kind you liked so I got the one that smelled the best. She tossed the pouch across the room to her. Mary Ellen's eyes lit up when she opened it.

"Mrs. Margaret Harrison! I don't deserve this, thank you." She took a deep breath of the pouch. "Get your coat on. We're going for a walk."

"You've got dinner in twenty minutes, Miss."

"I don't care," she said, scrambling to put on her jacket and gloves. "I'll smoke it in the fireplace."

"No, no, no. You put on these old shite gloves and the dress from yesterday. I won't have you at dinner smelling of pipe," Margaret said, getting the old dress out and helping Mary Ellen into it.

A few moments later, they were outside in the back garden by the stables where they knew the rest of the staff would go to smoke. Mary Ellen stood there in her dirty dress and old gloves, wrapped in a wool blanket. She carefully packed and took a match to her father's corn cob pipe, puffing out the smoke in rapid succession to ensure it stayed lit. The smell took her back home faster than any steamer ship could ever hope to. She nearly cried as she smoked it.

"Did I get a good one?" Margaret asked.

"What was it called?" Mary Ellen asked.

"I think it was Burnside."

"I knew it, we used to sell to them."

"It's not your farms, is it?"

"We didn't produce a crop for almost two years. Besides, they blend it all anyway." Mary Ellen rummaged through her pocket with her free hand. "How much did you pay for it? I've got some money."

"No, Miss, it's fine," Margaret said. "But we need to get back soon. I've got to get you changed before dinner."

Mary Ellen nodded and stuck her fingers over the bowl of the pipe, puffed it out and stuck a small cork inside the bowl to keep it for later. They quickly returned upstairs to change. Mary Ellen made a point to sit opposite her mother at the dinner table so she wouldn't smell any of the pipe smoke in her hair, even though Margaret had done her best to mask it with perfumes and powders.

"We're going home next week, Mary Ellen," her mother said eating her barely still warm dinner. "Have Mrs. Harrison send your things to the cleaners tomorrow so we can have it ready for Monday."

"Yes, Momma."

"We have two more calls to make tomorrow, then we'll have a day off and we can go shopping if you want before we head back home."

Just hearing the words "head back home" struck a nerve with Mary Ellen. To her, home was in Georgia—her little brothers playing with sticks in the field while she and Violet shelled peas on the porch for the next day's dinner. Home was her father coming home from a trip to town with a bag of candy for each of them. Redbriar wasn't her home so much as it was a museum of gilded suffering. Cold floors, cold rooms, strange food she was certain had been boiled in a pot for a day. She had felt homesickness before on the boat ride over, but having the pipe earlier made all the memories of home come flooding back to her. A home that was gone forever. "OK, Momma," she acknowledged into her bowl of now cold soup.

"Are you alright dear?" her mother asked, suddenly concerned with the way her daughter was behaving.

"I'll be alright," she said, laid her spoon across the bowl.

"You should get some rest. I can have Mrs. Harrison bring you a late breakfast if you need."

"OK, Momma," she said.

"You're wearing the poor girl out," her uncle said, chiming in to the conversation. "She'll do fine when the season comes. I'll bet she snags a husband after her first ball."

"The first season is always for show, Edmund."

"I'll go with you tomorrow, before you make your calls. I can show her around the bank. See if some of my influence can assist," he said.

"That's a wonderful idea, Edmund."

Mary Ellen knew the reason she felt bad wasn't from making calls, but from having smoked her pipe for the first time in so long right before dinner. She kindly excused herself and headed back upstairs and made herself a glass of whiskey.

"You're back early, Miss," Margaret said, coming into the room soon after.

"There is a reason you smoke a pipe after a meal," Mary Ellen said, sipping her whiskey in front of the fireplace. "I think I'll go to bed early, Margaret. You don't have to stay up late for me. Just get these back buttons undone, I think I can manage the rest."

Margaret quickly got her ready for bed and began to leave. "I'll be right next door if you need me, I've got to finish up some sewing."

"Margaret?" Mary Ellen said.

"Yes, Miss?"

"Nothing. Goodnight, Miss Margaret."

The next morning, everyone climbed into Uncle Edmund's private coach and headed out toward the bank. Along the way, he went on and on about some of the well-to-do gentlemen he knew by name and had over regularly for dinner. When they were nearly three blocks away, a crowd could be seen forming, children and adults running through the streets. Her uncle peeked his head out of the window. "Oi! Lad!" he shouted at a boy. "What's this?"

"It's a run on the banks it is, Sir!"

Her uncle, being the thinnest man she had ever seen, climbed out through the window of the moving coach to his driver seated up top. "Stop, man! Turn this blasted thing around!" He shouted as though giving military orders. "Take them back to the house at once. I will send word when I can return tonight," he said, removing his jacket and hat. "Here, trade me your coat."

"But, sir!?"

"There is no time! Hurry!" he said, thrusting the clothes at the poor man and putting on his hat.

"Yes, sir."

And with that, Mary Ellen watched her uncle leap from the top of the coach to the ground below, his disguise several sizes too large for him. He ran to a back alleyway in the direction of the crowd.

"Alright, my ladies, let's get you lot home!" the driver called out. Unable to fit into Edmund's jacket, he perched his top hat at an angle on his head.

"But we have to make a call!"

"Not today, Miss. I'm sure they will understand."

Once back at the house, a crowd was forming at the front gate—a small mob of angry shopkeepers and business owners that had borrowed money from Edmund's banks. The driver instinctively cut back along a side street to avoid trouble. He stopped a block from the house and got off.

"Alright, my ladies. I can't take us to the stables either, you'll have to walk to the back of the servants' entrance." He looked at Margaret, "You know where that is?" Margaret nodded and the three were quickly out of the coach and on foot toward the house. "I'm taking the coach to a stable not far. I'll be back at the house shortly."

The girls made it to the back gate, which was so overgrown with vines it was a wonder they could find the gate latch at all. "It's locked!" her mother cried, exhausted. They looked through the gates to see if anyone was in the back garden, but it was clear anyone home was hiding indoors.

Margaret looked over the lock. "It's an easy lock, Miss," she said, taking two hairpins from Mary Ellen's hat. She worked quickly trying to pick it, but the iron lock was too strong. One of the pins snapped inside. "Well, shite. This won't do, Miss," Margaret said.

Mary Ellen looked around and handed her mother her hat and removed her gloves. "Margaret, my dress please."

Her mother stood in shock. "What on earth, Mary Ellen!"

"I don't want to rip it up."

Margaret pulled the outer dress up over her and carefully folded it in her arms. Mary Ellen went over and climbed up one of the trees that branched over the fence and slowly descended to the other side. When she landed Margaret began to applaud. Her mother hushed her, not wanting to draw attention to themselves. Mary Ellen unlocked the latch from inside the gate. Margaret and her mother rushed in and closed the gate behind them, propping it closed with a crate for good measure. They rushed to the back door of the house and began ringing the bell frantically. The valet answered the door and let them in, locking it behind them.

"What is all this?! Are you alright, my ladies? Where is Mr. Hadaly?"

They took a moment to catch their breath in the servants hall.

"There's been a run on the bank," her mother answered. By then constables had begun to arrive at the house and were attempting to break up the mob outside the front gates. Once they were able to make it inside, they were greeted by her mother and explained the situation in the front parlor.

Margaret and Mary Ellen went upstairs to change. "Damnit, I broke one of the bones," Mary Ellen said, pointing at the indention in her corset.

"Ah I can swap that out in a tick. Climb out of everything and I'll get it mended before dinner. Your other one is at the cleaners still. We were supposed to get it back in today; you'll just have to go without for luncheon."

Margaret helped her change into fresh clothes and clean the dirt off her hands and legs, but without the corset holding her waist in, the dress looked humorously wide.

"I look like a tree stump in this thing," Mary Ellen laughed. It wasn't too bad, with her small jacket over it. Unless she sat down slumped over it wasn't incredibly noticeable.

"It will work for now, Miss. You're young enough to get away with it," Margaret said, pulling out the broken boning from the corset. "You should meet your mother downstairs and find out what's going on." Mary Ellen agreed, and left Margaret to her work.

The lady whose house they were supposed to visit that afternoon was able to make the call to them, given the circumstances. She brought her daughter along as well, since she would be coming out in the season with her. They brought a picnic hamper of lunch, which the four of them shared in the dining room. The woman, Mrs. Brightly, was an old friend of her mother's, so bypassing formalities wasn't going to hurt their reputation in any way. It's also why her mother saved her trip for last. "What a day, Rosalind!" Mrs. Brightly exclaimed, going on about seeing people lined up outside the banks, being shown away by police. "Have you heard from Edmund yet?"

"He sent a note saying he is OK, but will have to stay at the bank until the area is secure."

"Well, if you need anything, my dear, do not hesitate to ask. When are you heading back to Redbriar?"

"We are supposed to be going home tomorrow."

"Well that's a shame. We could have had you over for dinner next week."

"Olivia, you are too kind. I should have you and Evelin over for a visit before the season starts. Get out of the town for a while?"

"Yes, we must!" Mrs. Brightly chimed.

Mary Ellen wasn't quite sure if either woman was being genuine when they spoke, or were simply going through the elaborate conversational motions that had been driven into them from childhood.

Evelin sat beside Mary Ellen and had been talking at length about all the parties they were going to be attending that year. She knew the names and places of everything by heart. She knew who was who and who they were related to.

"I simply adore your accent, Mary Ellen!" she cheered. "You're from Georgia, yes? Oh, it's a shame, the outcome of it all. But look at you now! Bless the Lord for second chances."

Mary Ellen bit her tongue, slowly sipping her coffee as Evelin went on for what seemed an hour about every little thing she could think of, and not once considering what Mary Ellen might feel when bringing up a subject. She was doing her best to ignore her and be as polite as possible when the front door swung open.

"Edmund!" the women cried out. He was accompanied by two policemen, one of which followed him into the house, the other standing guard.

"Do not let me interrupt your luncheon, ladies. I simply came to gather some paperwork," he said, tipping his at as he made his way upstairs. The women continued to chatter, while Mary Ellen tried to eat her tiny sandwiches.

"I'm simply saying," Evelin continued, unfazed by a man being led into his home by police. "With your blonde hair and that accent, you'll be married before the season ends. I know it's absolutely rude of me to ask, but do you dye it?"

Mary Ellen shook her head. "Tell me, Evelin," she said, putting her coffee down. "What fine gentlemen should I be looking for during these balls?"

Evelin's eyes lit up at the question and she promptly exploded with information, dropping names, titles, and physical descriptions of nearly two dozen bachelors they were sure to run into at a party. She warned Mary Ellen of a couple of gentlemen who had recently come into money and were not quite as refined in the social scenes, that she might find them unsuitable to take over her family estate. Others were penny pinchers, sloths, and a few who were known gamblers and couldn't be trusted with real money. Mary Ellen was thanking her for the information just as Evelin's mother signaled that it was time for them to go home. As they were leaving, the policeman who joined her uncle upstairs was coming back downstairs, alone. He tipped his hat to the women as he held the door open for them.

"All's well, ladies. Should you need anything, I've left a man to watch the gate overnight." Mary Ellen's mother thanked the policeman and said goodbye to her friends.

Uncle Edmund slowly descended the stairs, "Are they gone?" he whispered to the women. Her mother watched through the windows until the officer had walked clear of the house.

"Yes, he's gone. What on earth have you done, Edmund?"

"It's best you not know," he said. "But I need you to take something home with you tomorrow.

"Edmund Hadaly, I will not play pawn to some illicit scheme of yours!" The two jumped at a loud knocking at the door. The valet answered and let a small boy inside. "It's the laundry boy, sir. He says the back gate is broken?"

"Tell him to leave it by the door."

"Yes, sir." The boy and two companions loaded four hampers of clean laundry to the front steps. Mr. Hadley paid them and sent them on their way.

Dinner was a somber affair. Uncle Edmund wasn't his normal cheery self, clearly worried about something he wanted out of the house as soon as possible. He ate quickly and retired to the downstairs study where he kept his good brandy. Her mother went to bed herself, helping Margaret pack all the clean clothes in the cases for the morning. When Margaret went to load Mary Ellen's cases, she checked the locked drawer. It was indeed locked, but the key was on her writing table. She thought several times of opening it to see if Mary Ellen had brought the gun along, but wouldn't dare move the key or the contents, as she was sure to be discovered. She went downstairs to find Mary Ellen, who hadn't come back from dinner yet. She walked around to find her in the study with her uncle, having a brandy and showing him her corncob pipe.

"What a brilliant idea," he said, looking it over. "Americans are always so resourceful."

Mary Ellen saw Margaret walking past the doorway and waved her in. She poured her a tiny glass of brandy as well.

"Here Margaret," she said, handing it to her. She thanked them and took a sip, though it burned her mouth.

"The second sip is better," her uncle said, pulling out a series of old books from one of the walls. "Now, Mary Ellen. Mrs. Harrison. I have a special task for the two of you. I'm giving your mother only half of the documents I need removed from the house. The other half are going with you upstairs to be put in your cases. It's not that I don't trust my own sister with the task. I just don't trust her with some of the information. Her case is filled with receipts and ledgers. Yours here, will be correspondence. I urge you not to open the box until I'm dead, then toss them in the fireplace at the wake."

"What did you do, uncle?"

"Mary Ellen, promise me when you and your mother make a decision on a husband that he has a mind for money, as our family does not."

"But this house, your friends, and the banks?"

Edmund shook his head. "I may have never cheated a member of the working class out of his money. But, a certain connection at the Bank of England got me in my current level of work. I took a bad chance and ended up double-crossing him. I promise you he will launch an investigation into my personal life to try and get me locked away. These letters are the only proof of crimes they can charge me with."

"Why not just burn them now?"

"Should I make it out of this mess, I'd much like to be able to read them again," he said, biting into his cigar.

"I see," Mary Ellen said, finishing her brandy. "I'll take care of them for you."

"Thank you, my dear," he said, pulling out a small cigar box of letters. "The documents your mother has are worthless to the police even if she hands them over. I guess I don't trust her after all."

4

A Redbriar Christmas

The next morning, Mary Ellen and Margaret were double checking their luggage when her uncle met them downstairs. "Your mother isn't feeling well. I'm afraid I'll have to have my valet escort you to the train station this morning."

"What's wrong?"

"She woke up with a bit of a fever. I have my doctor on the way, but I'm sure it's nothing."

"We can wait a few days, I'm sure…"

Edmund shook his head. "I'm sending some of her hat boxes along with you girls, if that's alright," he asked, knowing there was still a policeman standing outside his front door.

Mary Ellen nodded and had Margaret load the cab with the valet while she went upstairs to say goodbye to her mother. Once in the room, she could sense something was wrong.

"Momma, we're headed back to Redbriar. You get some rest, alright? You've just run yourself out that's all."

Her mother smiled, her face pale and drenched in sweat. "Don't come any closer."

"I'll be fine, Momma," she said, placing a wet towel from the nearby table on her mother's forehead. "Get some sleep. We'll see you in a few days, alright? No calls and no cards until that fever is gone. I mean it." She kissed her mother's cheek and returned downstairs.

On their way to the station, several news boys were standing outside selling papers and shouting the latest headlines. Most were about the banks and the internal corruption scandal. A few others were covering a fire from the day before. Mary Ellen purchased a copy and took it with her on the train. The Times was certainly more interesting than newspapers in Georgia, when they had them. Nothing but war and politics back home. There had been occasional news of a county fair or some such activity but that was all gone after the war. She made a note of some articles she wanted to cut out and send to Violet back home. Skimming through the news about the bank failures, she worried about her uncle as well. Rain began to fall as the train left the station and did not stop until they made it to Redbriar.

Mary Ellen was glad to see her brothers again, and promptly dressed for lunch with them. The boys were disappointed, as they had created a picnic for her and their mother upon their return, but the lawn was soaking wet. She consoled them, and they set up the blanket and plates in the parlor floor and pretended they were outside as they ate sandwiches and drank lemonade. The storm continued the remainder of the day and into the evening. Tired from the journey,

Mary Ellen spent her day writing cards and returning letters while Margaret mended the underclothes she had ripped up climbing the fence and tree in London.

"If it's not raining tomorrow, I want to go to the village for some ink."

"You were just in London, Miss. We could have picked up good ink in town."

"You're right. I'll send a message to mother to bring some back when she is better."

That night, dinner was just as overly formal as it had always been at Redbriar: roasted pork with various breads, puddings, and cheese. As the desserts were being served, Taylor appeared to Lord Hadaly and handed him a small card. Mary Ellen recognized it as the same type of card her uncle kept at the house. Hadaly excused himself and left the dining room. Mary Ellen assumed it was something to do with Edmund's trouble at the bank. Lord Hadaly was gone for several minutes before returning to his chair.

"Miss Mary Ellen, my young masters," he said, firmly addressing the boys. "I'm afraid—" He stopped for a moment to collect himself. "I'm afraid your dear mother will not be returning home." The boys didn't understand at first and continued eating their sponge cakes. Mary Ellen dropped her spoon and excused herself while rushing out of the room. She fell to the ground in the hall, leaning back against the golden walls of the corridor and burst quietly into tears. This was followed by the sound of the boys crying after their grandfather explained the situation to them. Baron Hadaly went into the hall to ring for the nurses to collect the boys for bed.

"Was it typhoid?" Mary Ellen asked as he walked by, holding one of the crying boys. "I'm afraid so, dear."

The remainder of the year was spent solemnly at Redbriar. Her mother was buried a few paces away from her grandmother's grave at a chapel in the village. Christmas came and with it a saw her brothers leave for boarding school in Italy. This left her alone in the house with the staff and her grandfather for the next few months, until the season began. By then, Mary Ellen would be halfway through the mourning process and would be able to move to grey and white dresses. Unfortunately, during this time she couldn't attend any of the balls and would have to wait to formally come out during next year's season. This put a huge damper on everything she and her mother had planned. Her grandfather worried incessantly about her not being able to be out in society with his age. Regardless, he brought her along to London with him attend his state functions and give the rest of the servants a break.

Mary Ellen loved being back in London and was glad to have the extra time to acclimate to the customs and social expectations. While unable to attend balls or parties, she was able to receive the occasional acquaintance or distant cousin, and practiced hosting tea and luncheons once a week at the London house. She would wear her favorite lavender dresses during these meetings as they were just as acceptable as the black ones she had to wear every other day. Some of her mother's friends would send their daughters to

Mary Ellen's luncheons to keep them from other popular parties being held at the same time, and thus away from talking to men and young women they didn't approve of. This worked to Mary Ellen's advantage, as she steadily built up a reputation among the older generations of the upper class as someone who was trustworthy. Those closer to her own age enjoyed the "odd" food she served, as well as hearing stories about the American South. There, of course, were those who disapproved of her having anyone over while still in mourning, as well as those who were distrustful of her uncle. Evelin often came over and would bring other friends she felt would enjoy Mary Ellen's company. Afterward, she often told Mary Ellen of the various other parties and balls going on and who was attending them, not to mention the mountain of gossip she held on nearly every notable person in society.

Once the season ended and they returned to Redbriar for the summer, she and Margaret got to work at once on new outfits and a plan of attack for the following season. Mary Ellen had amassed a small library of notable people and eligible gentlemen, based on some she had met at the London house as well as others that Evelin had given her information on. She loved the summer and spent every chance she could outdoors when it wasn't raining. Often spending all day in the sun writing her letters, Margaret would have to go back inside to cool off.

"I don't know how you can just sit out there in the heat, Miss. If it gets any hotter, the Devil will have to wait on you."

"It's not hardly warm," Mary Ellen answered, sipping her luncheon coffee.

"Here's your letters and all," Margaret said, placing a tray of mail on a table, along with some sandwiches. "I'll be inside if you need me."

"We get that fabric I ordered in yet?"

"Not yet, Miss. Boy said it could be another few days."

"Who did we order that from?"

"Sherrod's, I think."

"Damn, I knew we should have ordered it from Eckman's. They had us those bolts of linen in two days after we placed it."

"That's because your grandfather's new riding hats were in with the order."

"Well let's order Granddaddy a new crinoline to go with my new top hat and waistcoat then."

Her brothers came home to visit for a few weeks during the summer, and were beyond grateful to have something for dinner that wasn't pasta. Mary Ellen had the cook fried chicken and had nearly taught him to get the biscuits just right. The boys had grown while away, and when they tried to disguise their arguments at the dinner table in Italian, their grandfather corrected their pronunciation. Mary Ellen didn't approve of the boys attending school so far away from home and told them privately that once she was in charge, she would find one closer for them to attend. Most of her plans began with, "Once I'm in charge," or "When I'm running this house," to which Margaret would roll her eyes or sigh, having heard employers talk about changing things in a house before. Margaret heard all about how she was going to be elevated to housekeeper and Mary Ellen would just handle everything else on her own. She simply nodded along, knowing full well that Mary Ellen would need a full staff to keep Redbriar running smoothly.

Summer came and went quickly. The boys returned to school, and the heat evaporated into the cold and damp autumn that Margaret seemed to flourish in. Much of the time, Mary Ellen kept warm downstairs in the library, where she could smoke her pipe and write letters. Preparing for the season once again became her full-time job. She had narrowed down potential bachelors from over two dozen to about four, the most obvious being the son of another Baron, who she had met at a luncheon the year before. He had made no attempt at conversation outside of polite smiling and talking about his race horses. She figured he could play horses while she managed the house without issue.

Two other young men were sons of Earls, whose older brothers were set to manage their fathers' houses—perfect fits for moving down to Redbriar without worrying about their father's estates. However, one was an insatiable glutton, according to Evelin, who never ate the same meal twice in a month. The other boy was decent enough, but brought along his mother with the deal, something Mary Ellen wasn't too keen on dealing with. The last one on her list was Evelin's own younger brother. Of course, she told Mary Ellen every single fault in the boy, but after having a few conversations with him herself, Mary Ellen felt he could be managed well enough to keep out of the affairs of the estate so long as she found him a hobby. The rest of the options were either the oldest son, who would want her to move to his estate and probably sell Redbriar off, or they were pretentious, alcoholics, or worst of all—simply not interested in her. There were several who wanted nothing to do with an American wife, especially one who was a former slave owner. Much of the working class felt the same way. She often found it hard to get service from street vendors who recognized who she was, having to get Margaret to buy things for her in some cases. For instance, the man in London who sold her favorite ink would often refuse her service if she went in person, but wouldn't refuse Margaret from buying six shillings worth of ink from him a year. Margaret found out later from another vendor on the same street that the man's wife was freed from the U.S. a few decades prior. Sometimes Mary Ellen would try to mask her accent when talking to street vendors in London who she hadn't visited before, in hopes of avoiding conflict. She once tried to use her mother's accent with poor results and found that it was easier to emulate Margaret's Irish accent when she needed to.

Christmas was somewhat lonely that year with the boys away at school. Her grandfather had fallen ill over the winter and was stuck in bed on Christmas Eve. She and Margaret invited the staff to the main dining room for dinner, and a few bottles of good wine were opened for the occasion. Mary Ellen brought up a tray of turkey and stuffing to her grandfather's room after dinner. He was still asleep when his valet opened the door for her and placed the tray at his table. From what she could tell, he looked to be recovering from what the doctors said was a bad chest cold. That was, until she saw the bucket of bloody rags near the bed. He woke up for a moment, grabbed a clean handkerchief and coughed up blood into it.

"M-Mary Ellen?" He coughed. "My dear, you don't need to come check on me."

"I just wanted to wish you a Merry Christmas," she said, looking over the various vials of medication on the nightstand.

"Oh, is it Christmas already?! Why, tell your mother to bring me up a tea, my dear," he said with a bewildered expression.

Mary Ellen gave a stern look to his valet, who insisted he had followed the doctor's instructions with the medication.

"He's three sheets to the wind!" she whispered angrily. Putting her hand to his forehead registered no fever that she could tell, which gave her some relief.

"May-Mary Ellen," he stammered, reaching for his glasses. "I'm sorry I couldn't make it down for dinner. Doctor said I have to stay in bed."

"Granddaddy, you need to get some sleep. The doctor was right to have you stay up here. Are you hungry at all? I brought you some food from downstairs."

"Well how nice of you, Rosalind. Is your brother home yet?"

Mary Ellen began to tear up as she watched her grandfather ramble on as though he was living in the past. She didn't have the heart to try and correct him, knowing he was on a stout cocktail of various medications.

"Of course, he is. Now you get some sleep," she said and kissed him on his forehead. Before leaving, she looked over the notes his doctor left and told his valet that she would be back to check on him at breakfast.

Back at her room, Margaret was arranging sheets on Mary Ellen's bed. "How is he doing?"

"He'll be alright. The doctor's notes say it's just a bad cough. Lungs are now clear and no fever, but damned if he isn't as drunk as Mrs. Parker was at dinner. They've got him on a ton of medicine."

"I've never seen her drink that much before!"

"Two beers would have you red faced just the same if you never drank before in your life."

Margaret laughed. "I wonder why she did this year."

"Maybe she is worried about her job. I know I'd be. Your boss is sick upstairs, his next of kin isn't married and..." Mary Ellen paused a moment, realizing she had never really worked a job where she wasn't somewhat in charge.

"Don't worry, Miss. You'll be fighting them off with a stick come spring. You'll be wearing my dresses, after all. They won't be able to look away."

Mary Ellen took a sip of wine from a tray of desserts on her table. "To your dresses!" she said, holding the glass in the air.

Margaret grabbed another glass from the tray. "To my dresses!" She took a sip and continued. "To get your arse married and full of babies." They toasted their glasses once more and had a few cookies they had made in the kitchen that morning.

Mary Ellen sat at her chair by the fireplace, finishing her wine. "This house really is depending on me isn't it?" she said.

"What's that?" Margaret said, putting the tray outside the door.

"If I fail, I can just sell the house to some other Lord of North What's-it and go live in some cottage in London forever. But everyone else here, they need me to keep it going. So many people work so hard for this place every day. Nobody else would keep the staff on at the rate Granddaddy pays them. Mrs. Parker's worked here her whole life. Mr. Taylor's, what, the third or fourth generation to run things? I can't ruin their livelihood. And you, if I fail, you'll end up slaving away at some old woman's house or worse, working all day as a seamstress for pennies at some factory. You should be out there finding a new husband so you don't have to sew my dresses. I mean, you're not that much older than me, you still have plenty of time…"

Margaret walked up to her and took the wine glass from her hand. "That's enough out of you tonight, Mary Ellen," she said. "Go get yourself to sleep now."

The next morning, Mary Ellen walked downstairs to an empty kitchen to make herself breakfast. Her grandfather always gave the staff a few days off starting on Christmas Day. Most of them had families in the village. Only a handful of stable boys, a scullery maid, Margaret, and Mr. Taylor stayed at the house, as they had no other family to go to. With her grandfather ill, Mary Ellen took it upon herself to make them a proper southern breakfast. Mr. Taylor came down while she was frying the streaky bacon. "Looks a bit overdone, my lady."

"It's supposed to be crispy, Mr. Taylor. You'll see when it's all ready." She tended to her biscuits in the oven. "Did you have the boys move that shipment in to the bedroom upstairs?" she asked.

"Yes, my lady, awful heavy it was. Think she will be able to work it? The whole contraption seemed highly elaborate for a lady's maid to use."

Mary Ellen stirred a bowl of eggs. "She'll do just fine, I'm sure. Which one of those jingle bells goes to her room?" she asked, pointing at the servant's bells. "Breakfast is almost ready."

"I can fetch her for you if you like."

"I won't have you fetching anything, Mr. Taylor. You're all off duty today. The bell will get her up. The rest are outside, right?"

"Yes, my lady. I'll have everyone gather in the dining room."

"Nonsense, the dining room is a mile away, we can just eat over there at the servants table."

At breakfast, the stable boys and maids thought it was delightful to have the lady of the house eating with them downstairs at their table. The whole situation made Mr. Taylor nervous and he kept reminding himself that Mary Ellen enjoyed cooking for them. When the meal was over, everyone brought their own plates to the sink and washed them.

Mary Ellen took Margaret upstairs to show her the present she had bought. The room across the hall was vacant, so Margaret had been using it to sew dresses as there more room to work.

"Now close your eyes," Mary Ellen said, unlocking the door. She led her into the room, careful not to knock into any of the dress forms or many boxes of fabric stacked by the furniture. "OK, now look."

Margaret opened her eyes to a brand new, black and gold Singer model twelve sewing machine. "Miss, I can't accept this!" she said, sitting down at the chair beside it and looking over its incorporated iron-legged table. "It's beautiful."

"It's all yours. Merry Christmas, Margaret."

5

The Southern Belle

"It's here, Miss!" Margaret cried out, carrying an elaborately decorated letter to the library where Mary Ellen was working. "Oh, you must open it now!"

Mary Ellen took the letter and cracked open the wax seal. One had to apply to be presented to the Queen and not having time to do so last season, Evelin's mother had graciously sent in the application in her mother's absence. She carefully read through the precise lettering, making sure not to miss a single word. "Thank you for... Her Majesty Queen Victoria... St. James Place..." Mary Ellen grinned. "I'm in."

"Thank the Lord in Heaven! I don't know what I'd do if all this work had been for nothing." Margaret cheered.

"Well we could have just re-applied next year," Mary Ellen said, opening a bottle of whiskey and pouring a small amount into two glasses. "We will have to send Evelin's mother a card at once." She handed Margaret a glass. "With a gift of something too. Hell, let's just invite them over for tea to start the battle plans. Cheers," she said, tapping her glass to

Margaret's before tossing back the whiskey and throwing the small crystal glass into the fireplace.

Margaret laughed. "Mrs. Parker will have your head for that."

"I'll clean it up before she finds—"

Just then, Mrs. Parker peeked her head into the door of the library. "Is everyone alright? I thought I heard something break, my lady."

Margaret quickly tucked her glass into her dress pocket.

"Oh, not at all, Mrs. Parker," Mary Ellen said, moving to block the view of her open whiskey bottle and pipe sitting on the table. "I dropped an empty ink bottle is all. Don't you worry yourself about it."

"Yes, my lady," Mrs. Parker said, giving the girls an odd look. "Would you care for some tea?"

"No thank you, Mrs. Parker. I think I can manage until supper," Mary Ellen said with a gleeful smile. Mrs. Parker left, closing the door behind her. "Alright, Margaret I've gotta finish up the rest of these letters and get them out before the mail leaves. You go upstairs and find those yellow gloves that were too small. Lady Brightly has the daintiest hands I've ever seen, she should be able to wear them well enough."

At supper, Mary Ellen told her grandfather the news that she was going to be received by the Queen during the season. Having finally gotten over his illness, he had been spending his days preparing his work for the upcoming parliamentary session. "That's splendid, my dear! I'm sure you will look stunning at the parties. Hiring a dressmaker for a ladies maid seems to have paid off well enough, even if she is

Irish," he said, noting how much nicer her clothes were in comparison to what she had when she arrived the year before.

"Yes, sir," she said, eating her soup making no mention to the fact her father was also Irish.

"The dance lessons and such working out well?" he asked, not honestly knowing what she did all day as he was just as busy with his own work.

"I believe they are," she said, putting her spoon down. "Granddaddy, I've invited Lady Brightly and her daughter over for tea this week, if that's alright."

"Of course, dear, do what you must. It was gracious of them to take you under their wing in all of this. Lord knows I make a poor chaperone."

By the end of February, Mary Ellen had perfected her curtsy and practiced both walking and the extreme etiquette of the event alongside Evelin, who had agreed to stay at Redbriar until the season began. Since she had gone through the process the year before, Evelin gave her every possible tip and strategy to handle the ceremony, including how to keep her feathers in her hair, how to walk backward while making sure not to trip over her train—since she had to exit the room without turning her back to the Queen. Mary Ellen had already submitted the required cards for the event and packed most of her gowns and equipment. Margaret had been working her hands raw altering clothes as Mary Ellen was losing weight from the stress of the event. Evelin's lady's maid helped lighten her daily work by tending to the bedmaking and cleaning of the girl's rooms so Margaret could finish her sewing on time. Being an older woman, this maid would often criticize everything Margaret did whenever the ladies were off working. The constant criticism drove Margaret to avoid the older woman whenever possible, often locking the door to her sewing room.

"I can't wait till she's gone, Miss. The old bat is driving me right out of my mind!" Margaret confided one night while getting Mary Ellen ready for bed.

"It's only for a few more days, then we go to London and Evelin will be back at her mother's and out of our hair."

"I thought you two got on well."

"Bless her heart, she means well and is helping, but Lord she is dense as a board. I'm honestly surprised the girl can read."

"Come now, Miss. That's a bit cruel."

"I'm just saying, she'd need lessons to prostitute."

Margaret laughed, putting Mary Ellen's evening dress away.

"That's not a joke. She has been courting some boy for the last year and yet asked a dozen questions that had me convinced she didn't know how children were conceived."

"These upper crust girls aren't brought up on farms, Miss."

"The bitch can rattle off sermons in nine languages but thinks kissing while the moon is full will have you expecting twins."

Margaret went around the room blowing out the candles. "Oh come on she is helping you, isn't she?"

"Yes, I know, I'd be knee deep in it if it weren't for her and her momma." Mary Ellen said, removing a glove to throw a few extra coals on her fireplace.

"And don't you let them gentlemen at the balls know you know anything about unladylike things."

Mary Ellen climbed into bed, burying her face into her pillow. "Right, nothing about the gentlemen's balls," she said, giggling.

Margaret shook her head as she went to her own room and closed the door behind her.

After Easter, the girls set out for the London house where Baron Hadaly had already arrived and set up his affairs for the opening of the parliamentary session. Mary Ellen loved being back in town, but the memory of her mother began to haunt her as soon as she walked through the door. She made it a point not to walk past the room where her mother had stayed, and passed away. Margaret unloaded her cases while she went downstairs to visit with her uncle and grandfather in the library.

"Ah Mary Ellen, you've arrived," her grandfather said, getting up from his chair. "I believe Lady Brightly is stopping by tomorrow for tea, correct?"

"Yes, sir. I asked her to send any further correspondence here."

Baron Hadaly walked over to a small desk and pulled out two letters. "Yes, my dear. These arrived for you this morning," he said, handing them to her.

Mary Ellen thanked him and took the letters upstairs. With her grandfather at the house, there were more staff on hand, and she walked past little maids she hadn't seen before. The kitchen had a temporary chef brought in, along with assistants. This made the cozy house much livelier and more crowded, almost to the point that she felt overwhelmed. Back at her room, she read through the notes that she knew were just formally accepting the invitations to luncheon the next day. Mary Ellen put the letters on her desk and pinched the bridge of her nose. "Margaret."

"Yes, Miss?"

"Have you unpacked my pipe yet?" There was silence across the room. "Margaret?" She looked over at the young woman, who had an expression of near terror in her eyes.

"Well…Margaret?"

"*We…* might not have packed it."

Mary Ellen casually walked over to her and placed her hands on her cheeks the way one would before scolding a child. "Don't lie to me, Margaret," she said calmly. "I put the pipe in with my stationery. The matches and everything are all in there. It's even got ashes in it." She moved in closer. "Where. Is. The. Pipe?"

Margaret began to tear up as her face turned bright red. "It was broken when I opened the box, I swear."

"Bullshit. Why did you take it out then?"

"I thought you was gonna have to do some work or something and I'd have time to run out and get you another one."

Mary Ellen let go of Margaret's face and walked back over to her stationery box. "What did you do with it?"

Margaret pulled the broken pipe from her apron pocket. Mary Ellen held out her hand and she gave her the pieces. "My daddy made me this pipe. He carved it himself, ya hear?" Margaret stood frozen, unsure about how upset Mary Ellen actually was. "I don't care that it broke—it was bound to happen. He wasn't good at making them. I'm not angry that you tried to hide it, I'm angry that you lied to me about it." She pulled several coins from her pocket. "Now, you will get your coat because you have to make it to Rothman's and back before dinner."

Margaret nodded and placed the coins in her dress pocket. "Will you be needin' anything else, Miss?"

"That will be… Oh wait, I need more ink, the good blue we got last time. You remember where they had it?"

Margaret nodded and opened the door to leave.

"Margaret," Mary Ellen said walking over to her. "I'm joking, let me get my coat. Uncle Edmund can take us in the cab."

The girls made it to the shops and back before dinner. Mary Ellen picked out a brand new butterscotch Meerschaum pipe that had the shape of an eagle talon carved around the bowl. They also stopped by the stationer for blue ink and more cards. By the time the girls returned to the house, they only had about fifteen minutes to get ready.

The next day, Lady Brightly came by for luncheon and went over their schedule for the season. She had written out a small schedule of events where she would chaperone Mary Ellen, as well as others that Evelin would accompany her to. The first was the ceremonial event of being received by the Queen, as it was imperative to be presented before enjoying the balls and parties that followed.

When the day came to be presented, the family cab was brought up to deliver her to St. James place, where the ceremony was held. Mary Ellen had dressed appropriately, wearing an exquisite white gown that Margaret had sewn for her, which was followed by the long train. Her hair was stuffed with the required feathers. She had to leave her belongings and coat in the cab while she was inside. Lady Brightly escorted her through the process while Margaret stayed behind in the cab with her things.

"Remember your curtsy dear. You've been executing it most efficiently during our practices, but for God's sake take your time," Lady Brightly said as they stood in the long line of other girls waiting to be received. They soon came up to the man who was introducing the women to the Queen. Mary Ellen's face flushed in anticipation. This was the most important moment of her life up to this point. The realization began to set in that she was about to not just present herself to the Queen but expose herself to an onslaught of attention by the upper classes. The man called out her full name—well, the name she and Lady Brightly approved of. Mary Ellen Murphy-Hadaly. Placing her grandfather's name at the end had ensured that her application was accepted. Mary Ellen walked over and performed her curtsy without losing any feathers from her hair. She could hear nothing but the sound of her heart beating into her own ears during the whole ordeal and was glad that she had skipped breakfast as she could feel her stomach clench up into her lungs. The smell of her bouquet was overwhelming as she waited for the Queen to kiss her forehead. Within an instant it was all over. She backed away from the Queen and left the room, meeting up with Lady Brightly.

"I've done it."

"Good show, my dear! Your mother would have been so proud of you!" She cried—real tears in fact.

After the ceremony, everyone entered the grand ballroom to kick off three months of balls, parties and events. She had to remember the parties had a purpose: She had been befriending the right people and giving her best impressions to gain the attention of a suitable husband that would cement her ownership of her grandfather's estate. Margaret warned her of how Victorian gentlemen treated their wives, but Mary Ellen was also simply looking for a strategic business opportunity and understood the importance of her position in the house. Anything else was a bonus.

Now that she was out in society, it was Evelin that chaperoned her through the balls and parties that went on through the season. Lady Brightly was always there to oversee the girls but was always on some part of the party planning committee that required her to be working during the events. This, of course, allowed Mary Ellen to be strategically placed at tables by young men they had hoped to meet and dance with during the parties. She met several fine young gentlemen through these social events, crossing out many on her list of potential options. Some were uninterested in her or had proposed to other young ladies in the prior season. The dance cards from her parties were filled with their names. Some also wrote addresses so she could write to them, but most were shooed away by Evelin for being too forward or having had a poor reputation.

At one such ball, Mary Ellen was greeted by a young man in his early twenties that she hadn't met before, nor had she placed him in her registry of eligible bachelors.

"Who's the one in the grey hat, Evelin?" she asked, sipping a glass of punch.

"That is Henry Allen, he has been away with his family in India for a while now. I heard they were back in town this year. If he asks, you should very quickly agree to dance with him," Evelin said, handing her the dance card for the evening. "He has been in India so long, I'm sure a bouncing little blonde like you will be just what he's looking for. I'll have someone introduce you."

Mary Ellen was soon greeted by Henry Allen who asked her for a dance later in the evening. "With pleasure, sir," she responded and handed him the dance card to fill in his name on the time slot he wanted. He politely bowed and walked back over to his friends, allowing Mary Ellen to look over the card to see what time he had penciled in.

"The third dance," she told Evelin.

"Perfect. The waltz—that's your best dance."

They were interrupted by another young man. "Pardon me, but may I have the privilege of a dance this evening?" he asked. Mary Ellen looked over at Evelin, who gave her the nod of approval, before accepting and handing him the dance card. He bowed and made his way back to his table before the dance began.

"Who was that?" Mary Ellen asked herself, looking into the card for the name.

"That's Thomas Morgan, he is a youngest son of Earl Morgan," Evelin said.

"He's the one with the shipping business?"

"Yes, he imports clothing and such. A good option for your estate since he has five other brothers."

"Not too bad lookin' either," Mary Ellen said.

Several other young men made their way over and filled in the rest of Mary Ellen's dance card. Most were about her age and intrigued by the concept of dancing with a "Southern Belle." But, more than anything, influenced by their mothers whose families supported and profited from Confederate trade. A handful of other young men were enamored with the color of her hair, as most of the girls were so similar in appearance with their white gowns and brown curls. She spent the remainder of the evening dancing with the gentlemen listed on her dance card and speaking with them a short while afterward back at her table. The only two she allowed to bring her a drink were Thomas Morgan and Henry Allen. Dinner was served around eight but wasn't enough to soak up the amount of punch she had consumed during the evening.

Evelin's coach dropped her off at the London house well after midnight. Completely drunk, Mary Ellen stumbled up to the front door of the house and was let in by one of the footmen. Making her way up the dark wooden stairs, feeling as though she would fall backward at any moment, she felt the need to be as quiet as possible as to not wake up the rest of the house, whom she was assured was asleep at this hour.

She made it up to her room and quietly opened the door. Margaret was sitting at the writing desk waiting for her. "Margaret, Margaret," Mary Ellen stammered. "Why aren't you asleep?"

Margaret yawned, putting down some knitting. "I have to get you out of that dress. Spent three months making it and I'm not about to have you rip it off," she said, walking over to her and getting started unlacing the back of the dress.

"You have to do what now?" Mary Ellen asked, holding out her arms as Margaret pulled the ball gown up over her head.

"Getting a little carried away with the drinks, now aren't we?" Margaret said, putting her clothes away and pulling the ribbons and such from her hair as best she could while Mary Ellen stumbled and wobbled around. "Come on now, just a little more… there we go. Off to bed with ye, Miss."

Mary Ellen plopped down on the bed, laughing. "Oh no," she said, as Margaret walked over to the door to her own suite.

"Do I need to get the bucket out already?"

"I got punch on my dress. Margaret is going to kill me."

6

Hangover Tea

The next morning, Mary Ellen was already up, soaked in sweat, shivering, and vomiting into the bucket beside her bed. Margaret brought her up some coffee and breakfast.

"You get that..." Mary Ellen paused before vomiting again. "Get those eggs out of this room."

Margaret placed the tray of food on the table, lifted the silver lid and proceeded to eat the eggs herself. "Better?"

Mary Ellen nodded, putting the bucket on the floor. "It's so hot in here."

"I haven't even lit the fire yet, Miss," she said, going over to the windows to open the curtains.

"Margaret, don't you dare." Mary Ellen curled back into the sheets and moaned. "This is it, I'm going to die."

"Drink some water, Miss, you need to get something in you."

"Just let me die."

"I don't get paid if you're dead, Miss," Margaret said, handing her a cup of coffee.

"Oh, the one time I wish it were poisoned," Mary Ellen smiled, taking a sip of the warm liquid.

83

"You did that bit last night," Margaret said, giving her a slice of toast. Mary Ellen bit down on the toast while she was still holding it and slumped back to the bed. She tried chewing but simply couldn't will herself to swallow it and let it fall out of her mouth into the bucket below.

"Take your time, Miss. Your guests won't be arriving till this afternoon anyway."

"My what?"

Margaret laughed. "Oh yes, Miss Mary Ellen, you invited two gentlemen to tea last night. Their cards came in this morning and both can't wait to see you."

"You can have them both; I'll be dead before luncheon."

"That's enough of that, Miss. We need to get you cleaned up." Margaret dragged the hip bath from her room.

"Oh no, Margaret, not now."

"Oh yes, Miss. I've already got the boys sending up the water. They should be here any minute," she said, setting the basin in the middle of the room. "You're caked in vomit and rouge. No man will want to marry the disaster I saw this morning when I first came in."

Mary Ellen drank some water while two young men filled the hip bath with cold water. Margaret had placed a pot of water in the fireplace as Mary Ellen had taught her to do back at Redbriar. She wasn't as keen on the cold or lukewarm baths the English insisted upon and would always pour a pot of boiling water into it first. Once the boys were gone and the hot water added, Margaret took her chemise and walked out into the hall. "I'll be back in twenty minutes. There is a towel over there."

Mary Ellen slowly climbed into the bath. It wasn't the full bath she had at Redbriar, so while everything from the waist down was nice and warm, her top half grew colder by the minute. She took the towel from the nearby chair, draped it over her head and shoulders and lit her pipe. Relaxing in the bath made her feel better almost instantly. After a few minutes, she was able to take sips of her coffee between scrubbing the sweat and grime from her arms and face. She was carefully rinsing the dried vomit from her hair when Margaret knocked on the door.

"Bath time is over, Miss." She walked in holding a fresh set of clothes.

"The water's still warm," Mary Ellen said, standing up to dry off with the towel. "You can use the rest if you want. There isn't that much vomit in there."

"I'd rather bathe in the Thames, Miss," Margaret said, taking the pipe from Mary Ellen's mouth before pulling the fresh chemise over her. "Your uncle won't be happy with you stinking up his rooms with this."

"They're about to be *my* rooms, if today goes well," she said, walking over to the tray to eat her now very cold breakfast.

"I can't wait to see what beasts you've managed to wrangle."

"They're both proper men. Not these spindly little boys still latched to their mothers that we've been hosting the last year."

"Ah, so you picked the two with the biggest whiskers in the room?"

Mary Ellen laughed. "You know I'm a sucker for a man with proper burnsides."

"You can't go choosing a husband based on his whiskers!"

"Why not? Half the men that I danced with wouldn't shut up about my hair. It's a ball for the Lord's sake—no different than a livestock show."

Later that afternoon, Mary Ellen was feeling better after having eaten some lunch and was preparing for her guests at tea. With her grandfather at the house, they employed a seasonal chef and kitchen staff. She assisted the chef in making a few sandwiches and cakes for the occasion, as he had to prepare for the dinner during tea and was too busy to do an elaborate spread without more help. She thought it also helped to be able to show the young gentlemen her skills on the plate. The cook at Redbriar had taught her how to do proper tea cakes, and while she knew how to make Victoria sandwiches with strawberry jam, Mary Ellen opted to use grape preserves instead, with the idea the gentlemen would enjoy it more. She helped prepare a board of smoked salmon, pickles, and cheese. Ham and watercress sandwiches cut into identical rectangles were the last things she prepared before she rushed upstairs to dress for the ordeal. Normally her high tea menu would include chicken or egg salad sandwiches, but her stomach was still somewhat shaky from the morning and couldn't handle the smell of boiled eggs.

Margaret had laid out a blue and white dress with matching hat and gloves. She had chosen the fabrics that best complimented Mary Ellen's hair, often holding up scraps of fabric to her face and walking off to continue working. She quickly arranged and pinned Mary Ellen's hair into the hat, leaving several ringlets of gold hair to dangle in front of her ears. "How many do you have coming to this tea, anyway?"

"Mr. Morgan and Mr. Allen. Evelin is also going to be here without her mother for once, and they are each bringing a new acquaintance who each know each other or something."

"If Evelin's mother isn't chaperoning, who is going to keep an eye on you lot?"

"Uncle Edmund."

Margaret laughed, nearly dropping the comb. "You're joking, Miss."

"Apparently, he has lent money to both of them and says they're both in good standing, as far as payments go anyway."

"Well, that's good," Margaret said and finished the buttons on Mary Ellen's gloves. "Alright, you best head down then, Miss. Off to the cattle auctions!"

Downstairs, Evelin was waiting in the parlor with Mr. Taylor. "Damnit, Evelin, you don't have to wait down here. You should have just come up."

"How are you even standing, Mary Ellen, much less going through with tea?" Evelin said, herself exhausted from the night before. "I only got up an hour ago myself. Mother handed me the card and if she had told me it was next week, I would be inclined to believe her!" She gave Mary Ellen a hug.

There was a knock at the door. Mr. Taylor answered and introduced both Thomas Morgan and his younger cousin, Beatrice, who had also been at the ball the night before.

"Mr. Morgan, I'm so glad you could join us," Mary Ellen said.

"I couldn't say no to such a kind invitation, Lady Murphy." He removed his brown top hat. Giving a slight bow, he looked to Evelin. "Lady Brightly, I must apologize for missing our dance last night."

Evelin blushed. "Oh we have the rest of the season for dancing Mr. Morgan." She turned to greet Beatrice and lead her to the dining room.

"This is a lovely house, Lady Murphy," he said, watching the girls leave. "I've walked by it so many times. Your uncle keeps it so immaculate."

"Well, I do my best, Mr. Morgan," Edmund said, descending the stairs.

"Lord Hadaly, it is an honor, sir," Thomas said, extending a bow.

Edmund greeted him with a handshake. "The business going well I presume?"

"Indeed, it is, my lord," he answered.

"Excellent." Edmund motioned to Mary Ellen. "Has everyone arrived?"

She looked to the front door. "Not quite, we have two more."

Edmund adjusted his spectacles and smiled. "I'm sure they will be here soon. I will see you in the dining room."

The door knocked again. Mr. Taylor let in Henry Allen and his good friend, Mr. Gregory Waterman, who just so happened to be the young man Evelin had been courting the past year.

"I do apologize, Lady Murphy," he said. "My cousin had to turn us down at the last minute and when Mr. Waterman heard Evelin was going to be here, he insisted."

Mary Ellen smiled. She didn't care who the man brought with him so much as he showed up. "Oh, it's more than alright, Mr. Allen. Lady Brightly will be thrilled you could join us."

The group left their hats and canes with Mr. Taylor, who put them away while they were escorted by Mary Ellen to the dining room. "I take it he found out that her mother would not be attending?" Mary Ellen whispered to Henry Allen.

He blushed in response. "Oh now, Lady Had... Lady Murphy. I must profess my innocence in this."

Mary Ellen smiled. "I don't blame him in the slightest."

Once at the table, and after Evelin had calmed down from the excitement of seeing Gregory arrive, they talked about the ball the night before. Edmund casually sipped his tea, all the while keeping an eye on Evelin and Gregory more than his niece. Unbeknown to Mary Ellen, Henry and Thomas were good friends, having attended school together as boys. Whatever Mary Ellen placed on her plate, the young men placed on theirs. Knowing she had invited them to tea, and the fact that she didn't drink tea, there was also a pot of good coffee on the table, which one of the footmen poured for her. That meant both gentlemen also took coffee, whether they preferred it or not. Thomas claimed to have a favorite coffee stall on Oxford street, to which he was a regular in the mornings on his way to work. Both placed cream and sugar into their cups and were surprised to see Mary Ellen take hers black.

"So, Henry, tell me how was India? I meant to ask last night but it's so loud in the ballroom," she asked.

"Well, being from America, you might have an idea of how hot it might be. But I love it there—beats the cold and dreary winters of London, that's for sure. The cities and people are just as busy and lively as they are here, but outside in the mountains." He paused to take a bite of the grape Victoria sponge. "You simply wouldn't believe the views. Such landscapes and the sky... oh, you must visit there sometime."

Evelin and Gregory were lost in their own conversation at the table, while little Beatrice was content to sit and eat three plates of sandwiches and cakes as though she hadn't eaten all day. Mary Ellen noticed this and grew concerned as the poor girl was rail thin as it was.

"That's enough of those, Beatrice. Your mother will have me flayed if she finds out I let you eat all these sweets," Thomas said, smiling. "Her mother is very anti-slav..." He paused a moment. "Anti-sugar."

What Mary Ellen didn't know was that both Evelin and her uncle had given instructions prior to the occasion for both parties to never mention the war in the States, or slavery of any kind at the table. Luckily, Henry could go on for hours about the beauty of India without mentioning anything else related to the country or its people. Thomas kept his conversation to all the latest styles and fashions that were being imported and exported via his own business. After exactly one hour, Mary Ellen's uncle stood up from the table and thanked everyone for coming. He extended the invitation to return in the future should they wish and excused himself from the table. Mr. Parker came in and guided the guests back into the parlor to collect their hats. Evelin said goodbye to Gregory and thanked Henry repeatedly for having brought him along. They each entered their cabs and headed off.

Mary Ellen went out to the side garden to relax a moment and get some fresh air. She managed to keep a few sandwiches and a single cake down during the tea but was still hungover. Margaret came out to remind her that dinner was going to be ready soon. Mary Ellen lit her pipe. "I'll take it in my room, if I can."

"You should go down for dinner; your grandfather will want to hear about how well the tea went."

"You're right," she said, tossing the match to the ground.

7

Whist and Wagers

Every other night there was a different party or dance to attend. Mary Ellen's energy seemed to go on indefinitely, especially if one or both of the young men she was interested in was in attendance. Evelin would act as the middleman, finding out which parties they were going to and on what days. Mary Ellen had endless invitations and could easily pick and choose which to attend. Margaret spent most of her days mending ripped dresses, and soon was sending most of Mary Ellen's laundry out to be cleaned twice a week. Depending on what young man would be at what event, Mary Ellen would wear the color dress that particular one enjoyed the most. Dark blue for Thomas Morgan, and a light purple for Henry Allen. If both were there, she would wear a golden yellow dress that nearly matched her hair.

One morning, Evelin had come by before luncheon to discuss what she had heard or if one of the gentlemen had sent her a card to let them know where they would be. "There is a dinner at the Overton's Thursday that both will be attending. Should I get you an invitation?"

Mary Ellen thought it over for a moment. The Overtons weren't the best people for her to be around. They were great friends with her grandfather's brother and she knew that her cousins would most likely be in attendance. "I don't know, it's risky."

"Come on, you know they will be there. The other Hadalys couldn't possibly steal them off you."

"Can you get me invited without them finding out? A last-minute type thing?"

Evelin shook her head. "You know that just by having the boys there, everyone will expect you to show up. Maybe you could befriend them? Extend the olive branch?"

"Anybody out to take your house from you ain't about to be friends. I can be cordial all day, but I can't ever trust them. I can just see it—they'll bring up some highfalutin business about English politics and make me out to be a damn fool in front of the gentlemen. Then they change their mind about me and go after one of them—either way they get a Hadaly," Mary Ellen said, her hand trembling as she sipped her coffee.

"I think you're over thinking this, Mary Ellen. It's just a dinner and a card game or two."

She gave Evelin a stern look. "Cards?"

"Oh yes, the Overton's are big card players. Half their parlor is set up for tables." She paused, smiling. "You can even smoke your pipe. Everyone already knows about your little cutty pipe. You aren't fully English, so you get a pass, so to speak. That is, unless you take up using your maternal surname."

Mary Ellen didn't once think of how the fact that she was half Irish was going to play a part in conversations. She also couldn't stand the idea of disrespecting her late father by dropping his name just to float higher in the social pool. "The blood matters more than the name. It'll change when I'm married anyway. What time is the dinner?"

Evelin looked at her card. "It's at nine p.m., with cards and drinks to follow."

"Well, you best get me in the door then."

"You need to eat more, Miss," Margaret said, lacing up Mary Ellen's dress for dinner. "I'm not about to take in a dozen dresses, and my fingers ache as it is."

"Sorry, Margaret. I'll have extra at dinner tonight. I've just been so busy lately and all this dancing."

"And all the drinking."

"You'd think that would fix the problem."

"Maybe if you switch to beer."

"Beer and potatoes—got it. What's for dinner?"

"Not beer or potatoes."

"Shit."

"Alright, off downstairs with, ya."

At dinner, Baron Hadaly seemed exhausted. He picked at his food and drank several glasses of port as her uncle talked endlessly about how well the tea had gone that afternoon. Uncle Edmund had nothing but great things to say about the gentlemen, doing his absolute best to put them in a great light for his father. Baron Hadaly knew the young men's families for decades and had no issues with them.

"Alright, Edmund, alright," he said, tossing his napkin to the table turning to his granddaughter. "I don't want you rushing into this, no matter what your little friend Evelin says or what Mr. Morgan or Mr. Allen attempt to rush you into." He snatched his napkin from the table and coughed forcefully into it. Mary Ellen gave her uncle a look, which he quickly returned.

"Well, Granddaddy, I don't want you to worry about me," she said, motioning to Mr. Taylor to assist him. Her uncle stood up to join in helping Baron Hadaly up from his chair. Not usually one to accept assistance from anyone, he didn't object to being helped out of the dining room. Once gone, Edmund asked Mary Ellen to meet with him in the library. "Let's let the staff clean up this room early. I have some things to discuss with you."

"Of course, uncle."

"He isn't doing well, you know," Edmund said as he stood by the fireplace in the library. He hadn't bothered to light the gas lamps in the room, leaving only the light from the fireplace itself. He handed Mary Ellen a glass of brandy. "I'm hesitant to bring in the doctor to examine him. Should he find anything, the word would spread, and I'm worried of what my uncle would do."

"Surely it's just his hay fever."

"Oh, I severely hope so, Mary Ellen," he said. "But you saw him at dinner. Parliamentary sessions tire him out, surely, but I haven't seen him this bad before."

"You want me to make a decision quickly, then?"

"I'm not saying you should agree to the first young gentleman that asks, but should you agree, keep the engagement as short as possible. I heard about this dinner you're going to." He paused to refill his cup. "You should know that I don't approve of the Overtons. Their finances are a disgrace for one thing, and I don't want to catch you gambling with any of our money at those tables."

"Understood, uncle," she said, sipping her brandy.

"I don't want to hear about how you played cards with your slaves back home either. The Overtons are professional gamblers; their friends are professional gamblers. Now, I'm worried why your gentlemen are even attending."

"Oh, Evelin said that the cousins invited them."

"Of course, they did." He slammed his fist on the table, shaking the decanter. Mary Ellen jumped. "You're being lured into a trap, Mary Ellen."

"I'll plan for it, then." She put down her glass. "I have two days. I'm sure Margaret can help."

"What about Evelin?"

Mary Ellen paused. "This doesn't leave the room, but I don't rightly trust her."

"Good girl." He smiled, patting her on the shoulder.

On Thursday, Mary Ellen took a cab with Evelin to the Overton's house several blocks away. It rained the entire way and her coat became so soaked she ended up taking it off once she arrived. They were greeted at the door by Mr. Overton's wife.

"Oh, Lady Brightly, Lady Murphy, how wonderful that you have arrived! This horrid rain! Get in the house at once ladies, please." Mary Ellen walked into a kind and welcoming home. The parlor was decorated with various sporting equipment, guns, and stuffed birds in every corner. Several large creatures lined the walls, including deer, bears, African antelope, and large cats. Two huge elephant tusks framed the doorway to the main dining room. As they passed by the ivory arches and took their seats, the girls were greeted by Mary Ellen's cousins, Benjamin Hadaly and Lydia Andrews. Both were at least a decade her senior and very finely dressed for the occasion.

"Why little cousin, it's so nice to finally meet you," Benjamin said, sitting in the chair beside her. The place settings were all labeled with name cards, and she was positioned between her cousin Benjamin and Lord Overton. Lydia was set directly across from her, with Thomas and Henry on either side. She felt trapped in a game of chess. Evelin was on the other side of Henry, out of speaking range of Mary Ellen and unable to assist should a conversation go awry. *Uncle Edmund was right about the trap*, she thought, and allowed her cousin to help her to her seat. Dinner began simply enough, with most conversation starting with simple topics by Lord Overton. He talked at length about his latest trip from Africa, and how lovely the hunting was.

"Have you ever been to Africa, my dear?" he asked her.

"No, my lord. But I have been hunting."

Lord Overton's eyes lit up in excitement. "What a delight! You must tell me all about hunting in the States!" Of course, Mary Ellen had only been hunting on her own land when food was scarce, and the only things she shot at were rabbits and squirrels. She made up an elaborate story about her family going into the mountains and hunting deer and turkey—things her father and brother did—but she wasn't going to pass up the opportunity to get on the good side of her host. It was easy enough to diffuse any notion of him planning a trip to their family cabin back home by saying it had burned down in the war. Lord Overton, being an older gentleman, was sympathetic to the cause of the Confederacy, unlike the younger generations. She could see the look of discomfort in her cousins' eyes as she charmed Lord Overton and his wife with stories of the South. The more she embellished them, the more they seemed to squirm.

"My Lord Overton," Lydia said, while the footmen began to serve the main course. "When was the last time you went hunting at Redbriar?"

"It's been ages, and your great uncle hasn't hosted a hunt since..." he took a minute to think about it while the roast duck was being plated in front of him. "Oh, it must have been '53."

"I'm sure cousin Mary Ellen could have something arranged for you." She sipped her wine.

"Now, I shan't impose," he said and quickly changed the subject. Mary Ellen could sense something had gone foul between Lord Overton and her grandfather at some point. Uncle Edmund warned her about them, after all. "Mr. Allen, have you done any hunting in your travels to India?" he asked, nervously carving into his plate of duck.

"I'm afraid not, my lord. However, I'm sure father can arrange something should you wish to land an elephant or tiger."

"Indeed! A trip to India sounds splendid. I must speak to your father about it sometime." He then turned to Thomas. "What about you Mr. Morgan? I know I've seen you out with the hounds."

"Oh yes, my lord, I quite enjoy hunting. Calms the nerves," he said, finishing his plate. "Might I ask, where did you acquire that lovely carpet in the parlor?" He gave Mary Ellen a wink as he attempted to steer the conversation away from her. Lord Overton went on and on about his trip to Cairo and how his wife had to have the Egyptian rug in the markets.

"I simply love Cairo," Lydia exclaimed. "My husband and I spent the winter there a year ago and I simply couldn't get enough of it." Mrs. Overton beamed, and the two women rattled on for several minutes about the shopping and food. Before everyone knew it, dinner was over, and Lord Overton had announced to the room that card games would commence in the parlor along with a buffet of desserts. By then, it was well over eleven p.m., and the heavy dinner was taking its toll on everyone's energy. Mary Ellen assumed this was Lord Overton's way of making money at the card tables: fill everyone up on heavy meats and potatoes then wipe them clean while they were half conscious. Margaret had given her a couple of pep tablets she picked up from the druggist the day before, so she quickly took one from the inside of her glove and snuck it into her mouth. Margaret often took them when working late into the night sewing her dresses and warned her not to take more than half of one at first.

"Now, what was that Miss Murphy?" Henry Allen asked, having walked up beside her on his way to the tables. "Oh, just something to keep me going through the evening," she said. The tablet worked quickly and she felt herself flush with energy, as though she had just downed an entire pot of coffee.

"I may need one myself after a game or two. I'm often in bed by midnight these days," he said, helping her to the card table. Lord Overton had hired card dealers for the occasion, something Mary Ellen distrusted immediately. "Have you played Whist before?" he asked. She claimed to have only dabbled in it, but in fact Margaret had spent the last three days drilling the game into Mary Ellen's head. "Then you shall be on my team then, if you shall have me?" he asked.

"Oh yes, I think that will be wonderful," she said as they sat down. Her cousins sat opposite them as the opposing players. The game began, and Henry Allen took the lead. He would often turn to Mary Ellen to ask her advice on what card to play, and she would flirt and point to an obviously poor card. He would smile and show her the correct one to play and proceed to win the bet. She enjoyed watching him humiliate her cousins, who were flustered by his card playing. Sitting so close to him, she slyly placed a hand on his knee, covered up by the cloth on the table itself.

"Trumped again! You are too good for us, Mr. Allen," Benjamin said in frustration. "One more game?" he pleaded.

"I never turn down an invitation to a game, Mr. Hadaly." He smirked, his eyes fixated on Mary Ellen.

The next game, however, went incredibly poorly. Benjamin stood aside for the second round, letting his sister play the cards. She won with nearly impossible suits. Mary Ellen assumed that they were being hustled from the beginning and halfway through the game, stopped Henry from betting too much. Any time Lydia was looking at her hand, Mary Ellen would tap his leg with her foot. He took the signal that she was going to play something good and bet more conservatively. They still lost the game, but he had saved himself the embarrassment of losing too much money. After the round, everyone got up to trade gaming partners and have refreshments. Henry Allen thanked Mary Ellen for helping him. "Did you know they were cheating?" he whispered to her.

"Mr. Allen, do not trust my cousins. Yours isn't the only fortune they are after."

"I understand," he said and placed his hand around her waist. "Don't let them rake out our Thomas. He isn't as good of a player as I am." Mary Ellen smiled, and thanked him for the game. They shared some tea cakes and a few cups of tea before changing up gaming partners.

For the next round, Mary Ellen was partnered up with Mrs. Overton, but at the last moment she felt too tired and asked if anyone wanted to take her place at the tables. She gave Mary Ellen a sly smile as Thomas gladly stepped in for her. He walked over to the tables and sat beside her. "I don't know how well your last games went, but I believe these people to be cheats," he whispered.

"Indeed, they are, Mr. Morgan. I say we lead them on for a little bit."

During their first round, they played Mr. Overton and Evelin. They let Mr. Overton win out of hospitality for the dinner and he took his leave from the table at the end of the round. Henry stepped in and asked if he could take over for him, to which he agreed. Evelin also claimed to be too tired to play and was quickly replaced with Lydia. Mary Ellen gave her a stern look for having abandoned the game so suddenly.

"Now, this should be an interesting game," Lydia claimed, awaiting the dealer to hand out the cards. Henry Allen sat directly across from Mary Ellen and every time they had a stacked hand, he would tap her leg with his foot. When Mary Ellen knew they had a good hand, she would tap his leg and he would suggest to Lydia that they bid higher, only to lose everything at the end.

By the end of the round, Lydia and Benjamin thanked Lord Overton for the dinner and games and made their way home. With just the younger group left, Lord Overton begged them to play one more game before calling it an evening. He brought out brandy and cigars for the gentlemen.

"Lady Brightly told me you enjoy a good pipe. I have a proper Kentucky tobacco I think you might enjoy," he said, handing her a small glass jar. Mary Ellen took out her pipe and thanked him for the tobacco. She packed it while the men lit their cigars. "Now, who is playing the final round?" he asked.

"If you'll allow it, Lord Overton," Henry Allen proclaimed. "I would like to play my friend Mr. Morgan. One on one."

Lord Overton applauded. "A gentlemen's duel! I like it. Shall we play, Lady Murphy?"

She agreed, mostly out of courtesy, assuming his dealer would hand him better cards. They continued to play though Evelin had fallen asleep on a couch by the buffet, and it was well past two in the morning. Lord Overton was sweeping the floor with her, every hand being better than the next. She quickly lost the little money she brought with her.

"It has been great fun, Lord Overton, but it seems you have bested me greatly," she said, puffing at her pipe. It was indeed good tobacco. Given, any tobacco was good after seven glasses of wine and two cocaine tablets. She pushed her coins forward to him, only for him to push them back to her.

"No, Lady Murphy. This was a game of goodwill." He motioned to Evelin over on the couch. "Your friend there insisted your cousins come for dinner." He whispered, "Between us, I'd like to mend the breakage between your family and mine. I'm sure your uncle warned you about coming here, and he had good reason to. I've done him wrong more than once and I wish to make it up to him." Mary Ellen thanked him for the gesture and assured him that whatever happened in the past would be behind them.

Meanwhile the gentlemen were still deeply entrenched in their game. Each move was being calculated with great accuracy. Mary Ellen and Lord Overton walked over to their table, which had no money at all on it. "My boys, what on earth are you betting on?"

"We are playing for the right to ask Lady Murphy for her hand in marriage," Henry said. Both men looked up and smiled. Lord Overton laughed, tapping his cigar, "What fun! Really what are the odds at stake?"

Thomas gave him a stern look. "No, my lord, those are the stakes. We are quite serious."

Mary Ellen blushed. Two men were playing a game of cards not to win money but to win the first chance to ask her to marry him. "Well, well, gentlemen. Those are high stakes indeed," she said, biting down on her pipe. They both pulled up their chairs to their table to watch intently.

The room grew quiet as Lord Overton nodded at his dealer. "With odds like that, I think a quick shuffle is in order," he said, and with that, the dealer took the deck and shuffled it twice with incredible precision. The rest of the game was intense. Henry Allen was winning but not by much. He was clearly the better card player, but with the deck now shuffled properly, the odds could change at any moment. The final hand was dealt. Both men played their last trick on the table.

Mary Ellen didn't arrive home until four in the morning. Margaret was still asleep, knowing not to wait up for her. Mary Ellen floundered into the bedroom and collapsed to the bed, trying desperately to unbutton her dress. Failing, she went into Margaret's room and woke her up. "Marg'ret," she slurred. "Muh Marg'ret. I can't this dress."

Margaret rolled over in her bed and unlaced the buttons on Mary Ellen's dress and undid the laces of the corset all without fully waking herself up. Mary Ellen stood up, pulled off the rest of the dress and corset together in one big pile on a nearby chair. She stumbled, trying to walk back through the doorway.

"How did it go?" Margaret asked.

Mary Ellen fumbled back toward her. "I have accepted the invitation to marry one Mr. Thomas

Morgan." She then walked back through the doorway only to stop again.

"What?" Margaret asked.

"I'll be needing a wedding dress."

8

The Happy Couple

With swift approval from her family, Mary Ellen became Mrs. Thomas Morgan on a very windy September 8th, 1867. Her uncle paid for their honeymoon to Rome, where they spent several weeks just lounging around the city and going shopping. One of her favorite things about Thomas was the fact that he was an astute salesman, which led to not just a good price on a new pair of gloves but also a supplier connection or two to make use of back home. She enjoyed every second of Italy—the food, the music, and most importantly, the climate. It reminded her of summers back home. Margaret and Thomas's valet, Richmond, didn't care much for the weather but did enjoy the trip just the same, as it was an escape from the monotony of their lives, and they had most of the day to themselves to do as they wished.

The jolting trip back to London reminded Mary Ellen that her home was now at Redbriar, and not Georgia any more than it was Rome. They were met at the doors of Redbriar by Mr. Taylor and Mrs. Parker, but rather than the elated smiles Mary Ellen was used to seeing, both were solemn and avoided eye contact

107

with her. "Mr. Taylor I would think you would be happy to see us?" Mary Ellen said getting out of the coach.

He shook his head. "Oh I am, my lady, I am. You should get inside and see your grandfather at once."

Mary Ellen's face went white as she noticed the black arm band on his jacket. "You should have sent for us! I swear—" She bolted into the house. There, in the parlor, sat her grandfather, sipping a glass of brandy.

"How was Italy, my dear?" he asked.

"What happened?" Mary Ellen shouted, relieved that her grandfather wasn't the one who had died, but now angry.

He sighed, placing his glass on the table. "I'm afraid your brothers fell ill at school while you were away."

Mary Ellen winced in pain as she tried to hold back the tears. "What happened?"

"I'm sorry my dear. We buried them at the cemetery three days ago. You should go out and see them after you get settled in."

Mary Ellen collapsed on the floor in tears. She had now lost not only her father, and mother but now both of her siblings. Her only remaining family sat in the parlor of the house—her uncle standing not too far from her grandfather. Visiting Redbriar was something he rarely did. Thomas then came through the door and picked Mary Ellen up into his arms. "I'm so sorry, Mary Ellen," he said, kissing her forehead as he made his way up the stairs and following Mrs. Parker up to their new rooms.

The staff had spent the last two weeks refinishing one of the master suites in the house for the new couple. Every detail had been attended to, which made the whole ordeal more somber. Flowers had been set on the tables, and new sheets and furniture were placed around the room. The latest carpets from India as well as several stacks of wedding gifts were awaiting them. Thomas brought her through the doorway, sat her down on her bed and held her until she stopped crying.

"It's going to be alright," he said, wiping the tears from her face with his handkerchief. "My poor Mary Ellen."

"Thomas, what I'm I going to do?" Her jaw trembled as she spoke. She looked up to him, waiting for some sort of distinctive answer. He just smiled and kissed her cheeks.

"You are going to take some time to collect yourself and have Margaret get you ready for dinner before coming downstairs. We can go out to the cemetery tomorrow after breakfast if you want, but we can wait until you are ready." He stood up from the bed. "I'll have her bring you a coffee."

Mary Ellen grabbed him by the sides of his waistcoat. "We have to have a baby."

Thomas was taken aback and smiled. "I don't think now is exactly an appropriate moment, my dear."

"My cousins know by now that my brothers are gone; they're probably foaming at the mouth as we speak. Granddaddy doesn't have much time left—" He put a finger to her lips to quiet her.

"I don't want to hear anything about your cousins or babies or anything to do with this house until tomorrow. You are officially taking care of yourself today. I will not have a nerve-wrecked hysteric for a wife." He smiled, "And if you're serious about the baby I'll have Margaret bring you some temperance pamphlets instead of your pipe."

"Thomas Morgan, you will not bring that trash into this house! How do you think your workin' class employees would feel if they found out their boss was on the side of those old biddies who want to shut down their pubs?" She smiled, hugging his waist. "Stay here with me a little bit."

"I'll listen to your political ramblings all day as long as it makes you happy," he said, putting his arms around her. "But I do need to help Richmond with getting settled in to the house sometime before dinner."

"Mrs. Parker will handle it. He is in good hands." They sat on the bed for several minutes as Mary Ellen quietly let waves of grief wash over her.

"Now, will you be alright for a little while?" he asked as she seemed to have stopped crying. Mary Ellen nodded, and let him up from the bed. Thomas left the room as Margaret came in with a tray of coffee and snacks.

"I'm so sorry, Miss," she said, setting the tray down on the table.

"Do you like this room, Margaret?" she asked, wiping her irritated red eyes with Thomas's handkerchief.

"Aye, Miss, much more room, innit? Mrs. Parker says it used to be your other uncle's."

Mary Ellen slowly nibbled a sandwich from the tray while Margaret poured her a coffee. Mary Ellen took a sip to wash down the very dry bread when she felt a familiar burn in her throat. "Bless you, woman," she said, noting the brandy in the coffee. "What time is it?"

Margaret looked at her pocket watch. "Nearly five, Miss."

"Damn," Mary Ellen said, looking over the room. The sides of the walls were stacked with various wedding gifts that had been sent to the house while they were away. "Let's get me ready for dinner then." She walked over to the window and looked at some of the gifts while Margaret began the unlacing process. One of the boxes caught her eye, as it wasn't as fancy or wrapped in elaborate paper. It was a decently sized wooden box with the address hand written in grease pencil. One glance at the script told her exactly who had sent it. "Oh my God," she gasped as she attempted to open the crate with her fingers. She pulled an envelope knife from her desk and pried the lid open, all the while Margaret was removing parts of her dress.

"Stand still. What is it?"

Mary Ellen tossed the lid to the floor exposing a box filled with a mixture of sawdust and newspaper. The wondrous smell from the stuffing lifted her mood. There was a tin jar inside, as well as something rolled up in soft light leather.

"Come now, Miss, tell me what it is."

She pulled out the tin jar, opened the lid, the scent of aged tobacco filled the room. Mary Ellen sniffed the shredded leaves; the smell was so strong she had to back it away from her face. "I think this has been sitting a while," she said, putting the jar back down on the table and reading through the letter attached to the side.

"Dear Mellon-head,

Sorry I couldn't make it to your wedding, but you had to go and have it across the damn sea. Momma and me got jobs working for a cousin in Louisiana. We sell clothes and shoes in this fancy dress shop now. Finally, good jobs that pay good money! I sent you some Perique, they do it like whiskey, putting it in barrels after they dry it and Oh! You will have to see! Just be sure to cut with something lighter since it's so strong. The last letter I got from you said you broke the pipe Daddy made for you, so I sent you another one Momma made. We send our love and wish you a long and happy marriage.

Miss you every day,
Violet Murphy."

Mary Ellen was on the verge of tears as she read through the note. "It's from my sister. She hasn't written in so long, I know they moved, but..." She stopped herself from crying as she put the letter back in the box, making note of the return address written across the back.

"That's great, Miss! You've been waiting ages to hear back from her."

Mary Ellen slowly unrolled the leather package. Once the handmade corn cob pipe fell into her hands, she couldn't contain her composure any longer and fell to the floor sobbing uncontrollably. Margaret rushed to her side, dropping the fresh dress on the ground.

"Now, now, Miss, everything's going to be alright."

"Everyone's gone Margaret. They're all gone." She continued to cry, clutching the pipe. Memories of her mother and father back at the house in Georgia, the fun they all had with her brothers before the war—everything reminded her of a time that she would never get back and could never return to. Her old world had been wiped from the map. She would never see home again, and those she held dear seemed to be dropping like flies. Mary Ellen clutched the new pipe in her hands as though it would float away if she let go of it. Margaret sat with her on the cold wood floor. It took her several minutes to calm down enough to stand. Her coffee was now cold but that didn't stop her from walking over and drinking two cups in quick succession.

Margaret went back downstairs to inform the kitchen that Mary Ellen would be taking her dinner in her room. She also stopped by Thomas's room to let him know the situation. "Sorry to bother you, my Lord Morgan. She wishes that you take dinner downstairs with the family but to come up to see her as soon as it's finished." He reluctantly agreed, but not before sneaking next door to her room to see her before dinner.

He knocked lightly. Mary Ellen answered from the other side. "Come in."

"Are you sure you're alright, my dear?"

"I will be," she said, packing her new pipe. "But I need one of us to eat downstairs with grandfather. He paid for our trip abroad and I want you to tell him everything about it."

"Everything?" he asked, smiling.

She pushed him in the shoulder. "Thomas Morgan, if you bring up anything inappropriate at that dinner table…" They laughed, and he kissed her.

"I swear nothing too terrible will be revealed." He smiled and kissed her again. "I wish I could eat my dinner upstairs in my underthings."

"The world isn't fair, Mr. Morgan."

He laughed. "I shall see you after dinner, Mrs. Morgan."

Margaret had just finished her dinner when Mrs. Parker brought her a cup of tea. "How is she getting on?"

"She's a right mess, Mrs. Parker," Margaret said, taking the cup to her lips. "It's such a shame—never seen her as happy as she was in Rome. Good on you to not send word to us."

Mrs. Parker nodded and stared at the floor. "That's not the only thing she doesn't know about."

Margaret looked at her in confusion. "Not the Baron?"

"A half dozen doctors have been by these past few weeks. Something to do with his lungs. Now, I don't want you telling her anything, Mrs. Harrison. Keep her spirits as high as possible." Mrs. Parker said, tipping sugar into her own cup of tea. She leaned closer and quieted her voice. "I know this is somewhat inappropriate, considering the circumstances and all, but our jobs are riding on your mistress producing an heir."

Margaret nodded, her mouth still full of tea. "Yes," she said just after swallowing. "I'm three steps ahead of you, Mrs. Parker. Before we left for the trip, I made sure she was properly informed on the matter. Given her growing up on the farm and all, she knew the basics but not everything."

Mrs. Parker sat back in her chair. "That's a great weight off my shoulders, Mrs. Harrison. Just be sure to track when she is unwell, and give them as much time alone as you can manage in between."

Margaret smiled. "They're newlyweds, Mrs. Parker. You couldn't pry them apart with a spade. Nobody on that trip slept a wink as long as those two were awake. If she isn't with child by Christmas, it won't be for lack of trying."

"That's good to hear, though none of this leaves this room, you understand."

"Of course, Mrs. Parker."

"If he, for any reason, makes a trip to London, you see to it she goes with him," she said, getting up from the table to attend the rest of her evening duties.

"Yes, Mrs. Parker."

Later that evening, Thomas made his way back up the stairs to their rooms. He had spent an hour or so with his new in-laws, having drinks after dinner. Mary Ellen was at her writing desk when he came into the room.

"You didn't eat your soup," he said, looking down at her tray of half-touched food.

Mary Ellen didn't look up from her letter writing. "I'll get Margaret to take it away soon," he said, tapping her pen against the inkwell. "She is downstairs getting me another pot of coffee."

"Who are you writing at this hour?" He opened the adjacent door to his room, where his valet was waiting to get him ready for bed.

"My uncle," she called out.

"He is downstairs. Why don't you just talk to him in the morning at breakfast?" he said while changing into his nightshirt.

"My other uncle."

Thomas rushed over through the doorway, still working on his shirts. "Are you sure you should be doing that?"

"No," she answered. "But I should attempt to get in touch with him after grandfather passes away. You would want to know if your own father had died, correct?"

"Of course, but your grandfather seems to be in great spirits. Given recent events and all, I think he still has some years left in him." He wrapped his arms around her. "We have plenty of time to worry about such things."

She pressed her cheek to his chest. "Couple more days and we can work on our little family."

He kissed the top of her head. "Then you won't be upset with me if I run to London in the morning?"

"Of course not, Tom. Someone has to keep this ship above water," she said wrapping her arms around his waist. "Let's get some sleep."

Margaret had gained the habit of knocking before entering their room back in Rome. She placed Mary Ellen's' tray of coffee and tea cakes on a small table in the hallway. Before she could knock, Richmond opened his master's door and shook his head at her. The two had become friends during the long trip and were keen to help each other stay out of the way of their employers' more intimate moments. "Oh, for the Lord's sake," she whispered to him. "You want a coffee then?" He nodded, and they took the tray down the hall to the balcony. The two split the coffee and tea cakes while Richmond had a smoke.

They stood out for several minutes before they heard the door creak open behind them. Expecting Mrs. Parker to have just caught them slacking off at their duties, both bolted up at attention. Mary Ellen stood in the doorway, her pipe clinched between her teeth. "Yall can go to bed. He's asleep," she said, lighting her pipe. "It's cold as hell out here." Margaret scolded her for walking around outside in her nightclothes.

"Go back inside, Miss. It's too cold to be out here!"

Mary Ellen blew three solid smoke rings off the edge of the balcony. "Aint' nobody out here, Margaret. Go inside and get some sleep." She looked over at the now empty coffee tray on the ground. "Did y'all drink my coffee?"

Margaret took the tray from the ground and handed it to the valet. "Thank you, Richmond, I can handle her from here." He then handed it off to a cleaning maid at the other end of the hallway before going back to his room. Margaret let Mary Ellen finish her pipe before walking her back to bed.

"It's my house, I'll go out on the balcony when I want to," she said.

"It's not your house yet."

The next morning at breakfast, Mary Ellen was able to finally catch up with her grandfather and uncle. She told them about the fun she had while in Rome and how much she appreciated the trip.

"After breakfast, I'll take you out to see the boys," her grandfather said. "Edmund and Lord Morgan have a train to catch if they are to get back to London before lunch." He then looked over at Thomas. "You don't mind, son, if he tags along, do you?"

"The more the merrier, Baron Hadaly. It will be nice to have company on the trip," Thomas said, cutting his eggs with his fork. As he ate, he constantly wiped his mouth.

"Keeping those whiskers clean is a chore, isn't it?" Baron Hadaly asked.

Thomas nodded. "I'm afraid your cook is too good, my lord. We shall have to invest in more napkins!"

Baron Hadaly laughed. "I shall tell him you said that. Everything alright with the docks, I hope? Not another Tooley Street fiasco, I hope."

Thomas shook his head. "All is well on the docks these days. Simply a matter of signing off on a few manifests and checking on some new ships that have been—" He stumbled for the word, "—been ordered."

"You sure you're alright, my boy?"

Thomas nodded. "Just a little nervous, sir."

"No need to be nervous with us now. Perhaps you should take a walk with us after breakfast."

"I'm afraid I must ready my things, sir. I assure you I will be fine once I'm back to my daily routines." He smiled, wiping the corners of his mouth.

9

A Conditional Response

Mary Ellen spent her first six months as Mrs. Thomas Morgan enjoying her life and what appeared to be a stable well-being. She became pregnant around February, while the fledgling family was in London. Her grandfather was so excited about the news that he threw a huge party that spring and invited everyone he knew for a grand dinner to celebrate. By the following winter, a happy baby boy was born. They named him Gregory, after Thomas's father. Mary Ellen's grandfather had grown very ill by this time and was confined to his bed back in Redbriar. But once news of the child's birth had reached the house, he immediately called for his lawyers to sign everything over to the boy. Both Thomas and Mary Ellen were extremely protective of the child. When Mrs. Parker asked if a nurse was to be hired on to feed and care for little Gregory, both parents snapped at her. Thomas didn't trust a stranger with his son, and Mary Ellen didn't trust anyone that could have been sent to the house by her extended family. She nursed the child herself, and Margaret helped care for him, for which she was compensated extra.

Thomas spent much of the week in London at either the family house or one of his flats near the docks. When a shipment was late, or something was wrong, he needed to be able to get down to the water as quickly as possible. Edmund was almost always at the London house, and if he was hosting a party or dinner of his own, Thomas would move his own plans to a fine restaurant or a gentlemen's dinner club. When Mary Ellen and Gregory were in town during the season, Thomas moved all his business dinners to his old haunts. Not because he didn't want his clients to know he had a family, but because he didn't like having the baby exposed to strangers.

Margaret often scolded the two of them. "You need to take him outside at some point; he will end up with asthma if you don't."

Mary Ellen agreed to take him out on a walk to Hyde Park once the weather warmed up. "After Easter we will see about it."

Spring was always a stressful time for Thomas, as the sales of fabric and ready-made clothes skyrocketed during this season. If anything needed to be decided upon that wasn't part of the business, Mary Ellen was put in charge of it. If a family dinner was planned, she would send a note to his errand boy or secretary in advance to ensure he knew about it. Often enough, by the end of the day he would come back to the London house exhausted and would collapse into bed. Given the season was only temporary, Mary Ellen did her best to manage as much as she could for him.

That year, she had planned a family outing for Easter Sunday, knowing he wouldn't be at work and they could take Gregory to the park like they had talked about. They attended morning services and had a grand lunch at the house with a ham, egg salad, and hot cross buns. Thomas and Mary Ellen exchanged large cardboard-egg-shaped boxes. His contained a new, hand-painted silver snuff box, while hers held a pair of pearl earrings. A third egg was placed on the table, containing a pair of children's knit mittens and a tiny stuffed bunny. After lunch, they went out to Hyde Park for a walk around with Gregory. Mary Ellen was concerned about the sun being in his face and kept repositioning a thin blanket over the baby carriage.

Margaret pointed out that he still needed to breathe and folded it down, so he could see around him. "There, look how happy he is being outside."

Mary Ellen pointed out that she took him outside at Redbriar all the time. As they walked, they crossed paths with various acquaintances, some of whom hadn't yet met the boy and were keen to get a good look at him. Thomas's worry over the safety of his son melted away as he began to feel a sense of pride from how much everyone was poring over the boy.

"He is just simply precious!"

"Oh, you must have him over to play sometime!"

"What a handsome little man!"

The other families were courteous enough not to touch the boy, but with all the attention, Thomas became so excited that he picked him up from out of the carriage and held him up to his shoulder. Gregory was so happy to be sitting up and looking around that he began to giggle and laugh. Mary Ellen gasped as he did all of this without warning. "Oh, be careful with him Thomas!"

"He's just fine, Mary Ellen. Why, look how happy he is to be out of that damned basket."

She did notice, and her worry soon faded away as well. Gregory stared out at the trees and other people walking around, slapping his hands at his father's whiskers as he quickly turned his whole body to look in any given direction. Mary Ellen smiled as she watched Thomas point at things around them and seeing Gregory look in that direction, smiling. She then pulled her handkerchief from her dress pocket.

"Here dear, you've something on your chin."

He handed Gregory over to Margaret and took the handkerchief to his mouth. "It's happening even after you've eaten?" Mary Ellen asked.

Thomas nodded. "It's nothing, dear. Happens when I get thirsty these days. Shall we head back before he falls asleep?" Mary Ellen nodded and placed Gregory back into the carriage.

Back at the house, with the baby fast asleep upstairs, Mary Ellen confronted Thomas about his condition while they were downstairs in the library. "Have you seen a doctor about it?" she asked.

"I told you, Mary Ellen, it's nothing. Lunch was a little too salty. That's all."

"It's been getting worse, Thomas. You're drooling more than the baby. Something isn't right."

"I think I would know if something was wrong with me," he said, heading out of the room.

"Twenty-four-year-old men don't drool like babies!" she shouted at him.

Thomas turned around and stared at her. "Mrs. Morgan!" he snapped. "I will go visit whatever doctor you wish. But you will not raise your voice to me like that again." His voice echoed against the bare floors of the library.

Mary Ellen calmly walked up to him and whispered. "And you will not talk to me like one of your employees."

His face turned red with anger, but before he could so much as open his mouth, they were interrupted by a frantic knocking on the doors.

"Mary Ellen!" her uncle's voice shouted from the other side.

"Come in!" she called back.

The doors burst open, her uncle emerged, out of breath from running down the three flights of stairs. "It's your…" He paused to catch his breath. "I need you to come upstairs."

Both Mary Ellen and Thomas rushed out of the room to follow him, assuming something was wrong with the baby. "I told you we shouldn't have taken him outside!" She shouted at him.

"It's not the baby," Edmund finally said, sitting down on a bench in the hallway.

Mary Ellen froze. "Granddaddy?"

He nodded.

"I'll send for a doctor!" Thomas said, rushing into the front parlor to find Mr. Taylor.

"Mary Ellen," Edmund said, tears in his eyes. "I can't go back up there."

She rushed up the stairs, her eyes burning to hold back her own tears. Margaret followed her from the second floor. "What's the matter?"

When they arrived in the room, both had to look away from the sight of the blood. He had coughed it up onto nearly every surface. His eyes opened, and his mouth quivered, curdled blood seeping out. He had stayed in bed all morning, being too ill to go to church or eat lunch with them. Edmund had also stayed home with him that day.

Mary Ellen tried to address him but immediately choked up. Margaret put her hand on her shoulder as she sat down on the bed beside him. He was so weak and frail compared to the previous day. Mary Ellen had just talked with him the night before about Easter eggs and the baby. Yet, the man before her was moments from his last breath.

"Mary," he stammered, choking on the blood in his mouth. She rushed to help him sit up and cough, but it was too late.

"No, come on, it's OK. You'll be OK," she repeated as she felt him slump back to the bed. Thick waves of blood flowed from his mouth as his gaze went cold. "No, no!" she cried. "Granddaddy!"

Margaret pulled her up from him.

"He's gone Mary Ellen, let him go. He isn't hurting anymore."

Mary Ellen cried out loud, gripping Margaret's arms. "He's gone. They're all gone." She looked up at Margaret in fear. "They're all gone."

Thomas then made it up to the room. Taken aback by the sight, he rushed to Mary Ellen and picked her up into his arms. Her dress and face were soaked in dark red blood. He tried to quiet her as she cried into his shoulder and motioned for Margaret to follow him back to their room. He was careful to set her down at her chair to avoid getting blood all over the bed. He kissed her cheeks. "I'm so sorry. So sorry." He said, wiping the blood from her face with his handkerchief.

"He's gone, Thomas. They're all gone," she said, shaking.

"And finally at peace," he said, holding her hands in his. "He's finally at peace Mary Ellen, his pain is gone, and he is with God now."

"But they're all gone."

"I'm not gone. Margaret isn't gone. Gregory isn't gone. We're right here."

"Don't leave," she said, holding onto him.

"I have to go downstairs to help your uncle. The coroner will be here soon, but I'll stay as long as you need me."

Mary Ellen let go of him and sat back on the chair. It was then that she realized how much blood she was covered in. "Oh God," she gasped, looking over at Margaret, "I'm so sorry."

"It's alright Miss," Margaret said, still clutching her own handkerchief to her eyes. "Come now, let's get you cleaned up." Mary Ellen took her hand and sat up out of the chair, the blood, now cold and wet, was chilling her to the bone.

"Alright, let's go," she said and followed Margaret to the wash area on the other end of the room. Margaret quickly removed the outer bloody dress, but even her corset and crinoline were soaked.

Dinner that evening was a somber one. After the coroner, the police, and doctors had left with her grandfather's body, the house felt empty. Both Thomas and Mary Ellen had signed dozens of papers. Edmund sat at the dinner table but just pushed his peas across the plate. "I'm sorry, everyone. Please, give my dinner to Mr. Taylor," he said, excusing himself from the table. Thomas and Mary Ellen sat alone, slowly eating their meal in silence. When Mr. Taylor came in to serve the next course, Thomas stopped him. "Have you eaten, my good man?" Mr. Taylor shook his head. "We tend to eat during the end of the meal."

"Take all this back to the kitchen and have yourselves a feast. The stable boy and maid as well," Thomas said.

"Are you sure, Lord Morgan?"

"*Someone* has to have a good Easter Sunday."

That night, Mary Ellen was up late holding a fussy Gregory. Thomas was asleep beside her, and Margaret was sitting at the desk chair mending a pair of torn kidskin gloves. "Go on to bed, Margaret. I'll just have him sleep with us tonight. We've all had a rough day."

"Of course, Miss," Margaret said and headed off to bed. "Don't stay up too late."

"Goodnight, Margaret."

The next few days leading up to the funeral were dark and empty in the house, despite the sunny days of spring beaming through the windows. Mary Ellen hated how bright and warm it was outside, as though nature was celebrating her grandfather's death. Both she and her uncle made it through most of the church service without tears, but neither could hold them back at the cemetery at Redbriar. Having to travel back to the estate wasn't much of a problem for the family but was a bit of a rush for the staff to get things in order, mostly due to the fact they had to receive guests and host extended family members who came down for the funeral. Edmund had to have a room set up, along with a handful of cousins from here and there. After a week of stress and sadness, the guests had all left, and Baron Hadaly was laid to rest. The house was empty again and the wardrobes went black. Everyone was in full black—a simple armband on a maid or gamekeeper wasn't enough. Even little Gregory was outfitted in a black gown. Months went by before anyone felt like getting things back to normal.

At dinner one night, Thomas was wiping his chin as often as he was sipping his wine.

"Have you been to the new doctor yet?"

"Yes, he said it was just overactive glands. Gave me a few lozenges to help with it, but they're simply awful."

"Gregory took a few more steps today."

"Gregory?"

Mary Ellen paused. "Your son Gregory? The child upstairs."

Thomas waved his hand. "Oh yes, sorry, there is a new worker named Gregory at the docks."

"Thomas."

"Yes, Mary Ellen?"

"I'd like you to see another doctor."

He then stood up and threw his fork across the dining room. "And I'd like to eat my damn dinner in peace!" he shouted unexpectedly.

"Thomas Morgan, what is wrong with you?"

"Forgive me, dear. It's been rough at work this week." He huddled back to his chair, his hands shaking as he picked up his napkin.

10

The Investigation

Mary Ellen had Thomas seen by nearly a dozen doctors by mid-summer. Every one of them dismissed his increasing condition as nothing more than the result of stress from work, or various other imbalances in the body. He was prescribed a small pharmacy of cures ranging from tablets before breakfast, to a small set of plasters applied to the cheeks at bedtime. The fact that none of these cures did much of anything to help his mood, or the now almost constant drooling, made Mary Ellen skeptical of the doctors she was bringing into the house.

Thomas was growing more and more preoccupied with his importing business, spending entire weeks away in London when the family was at Redbriar, and hardly coming home to the London house if they were in town. One day, Margaret took it upon herself to question Richmond about his lord's daily routines while the family was at dinner. "It's none of my business what our Lord Morgan does outside his own house."

"But you of all people should have noticed how he isn't acting right these days?" Margaret said.

"I will not tolerate idle gossip from a lady's maid, Mrs. Harrison!" he said, slamming his fist on the servant's dining room table.

The family was staying in London for a few weeks to get Gregory fitted for some new clothes. Margaret was great at sewing gloves and dresses but wasn't confident in the latest little boys' ready-made fashions. Thomas had a supplier who offered to have him outfitted at no cost as part of a shipping deal. Mary Ellen had even gone down to visit Thomas while he was at work, having no real idea of how a shipping business operated. Thomas claimed that such an environment wasn't the type of place for a lady or child to be running around, as the ships were constantly being loaded and unloaded with heavy cargo. "We can go down on a Sunday evening when it isn't busy," she suggested.

"But that's when the common folks are off work, Mary Ellen. The place is even more dangerous for a well-to-do woman."

"The common folks?"

"Aye. It's just too dangerous, my dear."

"We've driven coaches by the harbor—it's teeming with women and children."

He shook his head. "All whores and tiny pickpockets. You can't go down there."

"Fine, I won't go down to the harbor." She smiled, tapped him on the head and went to leave the dining room to have her after dinner pipe and whiskey.

"Oh alright, you can come to work with me," he said, wiping his mouth and tossing the napkin to the table. "First thing in the morning though, and you leave Gregory here with Mrs. Harrison."

"Agreed," she said, holding the door open for him. "I won't stay all day—just to see how it looks myself."

The next morning, Mary Ellen and Thomas set out in their private cab toward Millwall, where his offices and the harbor were located. She never knew how long his commute really was at this hour with so many other cabs, stations, and buses crowding the streets. "I didn't realize it took so long to get out here," Mary Ellen exclaimed as they inched along the busy road.

"I used to have an apartment nearby that I would stay the night at during the busy season," he said, fiddling with his hat. His hands began to shake as they drew closer.

"Ah yes, I'm sure those wild nights with the local girls really helped at the end of the day." She smiled. His face turned red in embarrassment.

"Now, now, that's all behind me."

Mary Ellen laughed. "I'm not a fool, Thomas. I know what those red drapes mean in the windows of those 'hotels'."

"Well, you shouldn't talk about such things," he said, "Especially in public."

"Well, next time don't have the bill sent to the house."

"Damn!" he winced. "Which one was it?"

"They didn't say. I simply paid the boy and he carted off, but I don't want the staff chattering about such things. Send the bill to your office or have the sense to bring enough coin with you next time. Just don't go bringing them to the house," she said, holding his shaking hand.

"Oh, come on then. What if I pick you out a real good one?" He giggled, kissing her neck.

"Thomas Morgan, I will jump right out of this moving cab."

"You aren't angry at me then?"

"I knew exactly who I was getting married to," she said, "Which is why this nervous imbalance of yours has me so worried."

Back at the house, Margaret was putting Gregory to bed when she heard Richmond leave the adjacent room. She waited for him to finish descending the stairs before opening the connecting door. Once inside, she tip-toed to a wardrobe and quickly felt through several jacket pockets. Nothing out of the ordinary: a penny, bus ticket stub, and a button. She then went over to his dressing table and carefully opened the drawers, making sure not to disturb the shaving equipment and combs. She found the snuffbox Mary Ellen had given him at Easter and quickly opened it. Inside was a mass of dried tobacco. She put it away, disappointed to not find anything out of the ordinary anywhere. Before she turned around to leave, she checked the pocket of a pair of trousers Richmond had set out to be pressed later that day. She pulled out a glass bottle with a dirty paper label claiming to treat melancholy.

What on earth does he have to be melancholy about? She thought to herself as she popped the small cork from the bottle to get a better look at what was inside. Margaret tipped a dozen tiny, hand-rolled grey pills into the palm of her hand. The label claimed they contained, among other things, opium 55%, peppermint oil 5%, and blue mass 40%. "He's driven himself mad!" she whispered, then pocketed the medication into her own apron before quickly exiting the room.

When Mary Ellen returned that afternoon from her trip to the harbor, she was exhausted from the long cab ride. Gregory was up and eager to play, so she and Margaret took him out into the garden for tea.

"How goes the shipping business?" Margaret asked.

"Just as you'd expect a shipping business to be," Mary Ellen answered, stirring her coffee. "Lots of men shouting at each other in order not to drop crates of goods. Smelly docks, mountains of God knows what stacked on barges. It's not for weak men, that's for sure."

"But he works in the offices, right?"

"He has a small army of accountants and workmen going through manifests and orders across from the actual boats. I did my best not to get in the way."

"So it's a high-stress type of place, then?"

"Just as much as any workplace I'd assume," Mary Ellen said, sipping her coffee. "I mean, the other men seemed in good spirits, but nobody was being accosted at nine in the morning."

"You don't think it's the stress, do you?" Margaret asked.

"You know I don't, but I'm not about to inflame the situation just yet." She pulled her pipe from her dress pocket. "My sister is coming to visit next month, and I have to get the house ready."

"Is she really?" Margaret perked up, fumbling with the glass bottle in her pocket. "I thought she couldn't get time off from the restaurant."

"Her husband bought the restaurant after part of it burned down. She is coming to visit while he oversees the repairs."

"Oh no. Will it be mended quickly?"

Mary Ellen smiled. "It had better. I'm the one who sent money to get it fixed." She took a bite from one of the tea cakes. "She says she doesn't like it when I send her money, but she doesn't exactly send it back either."

"You think they are treating her right over there?"

"I know they aren't—that's why I send money. Uncle Edmund has it converted and transferred over and such for me." She paused. "Did you find out anything from Richmond?"

Margaret shook her head. "No, but he was very defensive about it when I asked. I'm sure it's bothering him as well, Miss."

Mary Ellen stood up, putting her coffee cup back on the tray. "That's a shame, I thought he had taking a liking to you."

"Aye, that he might, but not enough to risk his job." Margaret picked up the tray and followed Mary Ellen and Gregory back inside. As she walked, she whispered, "But I did find something in his room."

Mary Ellen paused, without turning around. "Of course, Mrs. Harrison. I shall meet you back upstairs when you are finished," she said, loud enough for the other servants and maids to hear her.

Once back upstairs, Mary Ellen put Gregory down for a nap and waited for Margaret to come back to the room. She did so with a stack of freshly folded clothes.

"Well?" Mary Ellen asked while seated at her desk. Margaret placed the clothes on the bed and pulled the vial from her apron pocket, tossing it across the room to her.

"I snuck in after Richmond went downstairs, found these in Lord Morgan's trouser pockets."

Mary Ellen turned the glass bottle around in her fingers. "Dr. Brighton's Tablets. For melancholy? Since when has he ever been melancholy?"

"I asked Mr. Taylor if he had heard of such a medicine, says Brighton's isn't really for cheering folks up. Those are for syphilis."

Mary Ellen's eyes grew wide, nearly dropping the glass bottle on the floor. "What?"

"I'm sorry, Miss."

"That can't be right." Mary Ellen was shouting now. "He's seen half a dozen different doctors this year alone! He hasn't had so much as a cold or sore in the entire time I've known him!"

Margaret rushed over to her. "You'll wake up the baby, Miss!" Margaret watched as Mary Ellen scrambled to unlock the drawer from her desk. "No, no! You don't know that's what it is!"

"I don't care," she said, pulling her revolver from the back of a stack of papers.

"They'll hang you if you do this, Mary Ellen!" Margaret shouted back.

Mary Ellen looked down at the gun in her hand. She was still crouched on the floor by the desk. "Then we do it so it's not a murder. I don't have any bullets for it anyway."

"We? Now, you can't go bringing me into this!"

"Oh, you most absolutely are in this," Mary Ellen said, standing up.

"I won't be a part of a murder."

Mary Ellen walked over to her, "You've seen folks who get syphilis?" Margaret nodded. "It's not a murder if you're putting someone out of their misery, and I'm not about to let him poison himself to death and drive us mad in the process."

"But what if he's well!? What if he is just taking it like the label says?" Margaret asked. Mary Ellen took the gun and removed a bullet from the chamber. Margaret jumped back in shock. "You said you didn't have any."

"I don't have enough," she said, handing the single cartridge to her.

The London house was quiet for the next few days. Thomas would leave in the morning after breakfast and come back before dinner. Mary Ellen would take Gregory out on walks while the sun was out. Everything ran like clockwork for a solid week. Not once did Mary Ellen mention the pills to him, nor did she watch to see if he ever took one when she was around.

Then, one day it rained. Thomas had trouble sleeping that night and kept her awake, causing breakfast the next day to be a tense meal.

"Why can't you drink proper bloody tea in the morning?" he asked her, clearly upset. "You aren't in America anymore. You haven't lived there in bloody years and yet, here you are, still trying to hold onto this shitty cup of black swill that stinks up my breakfast every damned morning!"

Mary Ellen stared at him in shock, as he had never complained before. Uncle Edmund nearly dropped his toast. "Look now boy, you will apologize to my niece immediately!"

Thomas took his full plate of food and threw it right at him. "How dare you speak to me in such a way in my own fucking house!" he shouted back.

Edmund stood up, enraged. Mary Ellen had never seen him angry before. "Your house? Your house!" He stopped to call Mr. Taylor over into the room. "Get this belligerent fool out of my sight immediately." Mr. Taylor went to grab Thomas by the arm and quickly had to dodge a fist.

"Don't you touch me!" Thomas shouted, drool running down his face.

Mary Ellen stood up from her seat at the table to face him. "Thomas Morgan! What in God's good earth are you doing!"

"Gather your things, dear. I want you and my son out of this Molly-House and back at Redbriar by the end of the day."

Mary Ellen seethed, grabbed her cup of coffee and threw it in his face. The hot liquid sent him tumbling to the ground, shouting every insult in his head before he went into a shaking fit of a seizure. Mr. Taylor and Edmund rushed over to keep him from hurting himself on the furniture. Mary Ellen called for Mrs. Parker to get a doctor. Thomas fought and screamed as the two men did their best to restrain him.

"Hold his arms," Uncle Edmund instructed as he wrapped his bony arm under Thomas's neck and squeezed until he went completely limp. Mr. Taylor lifted Thomas up onto his shoulder and carried him upstairs. Richmond met them at the door and helped get him onto the bed.

"What happened!?"

"He went into a rage at breakfast, then fell to the floor into a spasm. Has he had spells like this before?" Mr. Taylor asked.

Richmond shook his head. "He has been going through moods lately. Knocked a few teeth out of one of the dockworkers yesterday. Was told not to tell anyone but, I'm afraid this is serious, Mr. Taylor."

Thomas was awakened by the overwhelming odor of smelling salts.

"There he is. Hello there, lad," the cherry-cheeked doctor exclaimed.

"Who are you?" Thomas asked in a daze.

"You've had a bit of a spell, it seems. Made a right mess of breakfast according to Lord Hadaly."

Thomas couldn't remember ever going to breakfast. It took him a moment to recognize the room he was in as well. "I don't understand," he said. The doctor took out a rag and wiped Thomas's mouth with it. He then pulled out a new bottle of blue mass tablets from his coat pocket.

"Your valet handed me these in the strictest confidence," he said, showing him the bottle. "You realize these will drive you straight mad, don't you?" The doctor paused for a moment, making notes in his little booklet. "Now, you have a loving wife and

140

beautiful baby boy to take care of and you can't do that from an asylum. I'm going to prescribe you something else for your troubles that should still help with the mood swings. There is no reason for you to be in such a state."

Thomas nodded and pinched the bridge of his nose. "Is my wife still here?" he asked.

"I believe she is still downstairs, yes. I'll send her up on my way out if you wish." The doctor began gathering his things. "Shall I tell her of your condition, sir, or would you like to?"

"No. I don't want to be the cause of her worries."

"I believe it's a bit late for that, my lord. Call on me again if the new pills don't work for you. I've left my card with your man. Good afternoon."

"Afternoon?" Thomas thought to himself. He could now vaguely remember sitting down for breakfast, but not much else. The cloudy sky made it even harder to see if it was early morning or late evening. His mind was so scrambled, he couldn't tell if he was drifting back to sleep or catching himself waking up. The smell of pipe tobacco suddenly filled the room, and as if out of nowhere, Mary Ellen appeared beside him. She let out a frustrated sigh and took the pipe from her teeth.

"So, which is it?"

"My Mary Ellen. I'm so sorry, what happened?"

Unfazed by the sincerity of his question, she continued, "Why are you taking these pills?"

"It's nothing. I don't want you to worry about it."

"This has gone far beyond that, Thomas." She puffed her pipe, "I know about your little pills. I know what they're used for. I'm not a fool—you will not treat me like one."

Thomas began to laugh.

"The hell is wrong with you?"

"They aren't for syphilis," Thomas said, still giggling. "I did get them on recommendation from an old friend who did have it. Poor sod." He sat up from the bed. "What happened to me this morning?"

"Well," she said, sitting down on the bed beside him. "First you threw my coffee across the dining room. Then you got in an argument with Uncle Edmund and you called him a sodomite."

Thomas groaned in embarrassment.

"To his face."

"I'm so sorry, Mary Ellen," he said. "I didn't realize it was getting so bad."

"Why are you taking the pills?"

"Selfish reasons. I hate running father's shipping business. He sent me to school for this grand education, only to have me bark orders at dock workers all day. My brothers run estates, have half a dozen sons, horses, the whole lot. I have crates of linen and boxes of hats I sell to local merchants."

Mary Ellen took his hand. "Most people would see that as quite successful, Thomas."

"I know. I got used to living in town—the dinner clubs and women. That was the only thing keeping me happy at the time. A proper cut of pork and a savory redhead before calling it a day."

"You still do all of that. So, why are you poisoning yourself?"

Thomas looked over at her. She had the most unforgiving stare on her face. No story he could come up with was going to move her into any sort of emotional response. She had told him of her life on the farm in Georgia long ago; whining about how he hated his job wasn't going to help his cause. "My friend—who did catch it—told me the pills made him feel happy even though he knew he was going to die. I wanted to feel happy again too, so I started taking them. They worked, for a while. You have to take more over time to get the same effect, you see—"

Mary Ellen stopped him, placing her hand on his shoulder. "What did the doctor say?"

"He just gave me different pills to take."

"Where are they?"

Thomas pointed to the bedside table where the new vial was sitting. She looked over the label. "These are only different in color, some extra ingredients. I don't trust this," she said, putting the pills down. "Do I not make you happy? Does having Redbriar and Gregory not change things for you?"

"They do, but it's just not the same." He sat up from the bed, his head pounding. "Tell me, dear, do you think everyone will forgive me?"

"It depends if you can wean yourself from this poison. Without you, Gregory will end up as one of the dock workers you complain about." She helped him over to his wardrobe and changed his ruined shirt and jacket. "Go downstairs and get something to eat. I'll be down in a minute," she said, combing his hair and whiskers back in place and kissing him on the cheek.

The moment he left the room and the door closed, Margaret rolled out from under the bed. "Well?" Mary Ellen asked. "What did he tell the doctor?"

"He's tellin' the truth, Miss. That or he is lying to the doctor too."

11

Beyond Hope

Over the next few weeks, life at the London house was calm. Thomas was doing well again and was trying to be kinder to everyone in the house. Mary Ellen checked the pill bottles every night after he went to sleep to ensure he wasn't taking too many or too few. When her sister Violet arrived at the London house one sunny afternoon, she was finally calm enough to be excited about seeing her. While they had written over the years, she hadn't seen her half-sister since she left Georgia.

Mr. Taylor was the first to greet Violet at the door to the house. At first, he was taken aback by her appearance, as Mary Ellen hadn't told anyone that her half-sister was mixed race, but she looked so similar to her sister that there was no denying who she was. While she had darker skin and her hair was a wavy light brown, she shared Mary Ellen's green eyes and freckled cheeks.

"You must be Lady Morgan's sister. Come in. We have been most anxiously awaiting your arrival," he said, helping her into the parlor with her bags. "Mrs. Parker is our housekeeper and will show you to your room."

"Thank you, sir," Violet said, wearily allowing him to take her suitcases up the stairs.

"You must be Mrs. Pierroux," Mrs. Parker said. "Please, come with me. I'm afraid your sister is out with the baby right now but will be back shortly. How as your trip?"

Violet was distracted by the opulence of the house and stairs she was ascending. "It was the longest I've been on a boat, Mrs. Parker, but everyone has been nothing but kind to me since I set foot here."

"That's good to hear," Mrs. Parker said as she rummaged through the keys to find the one for the guest bedroom. "Here we are, dear. If you need anything, please let us know. The bell is over on the wall here." She pointed to a handle by the door. "Lady Morgan should be home any moment. I can have a coffee tray sent up if you would like?"

"I would love a coffee, Mrs. Taylor. Thank you," Violet said, taking in the details of the bedroom. She had worked in nice houses on occasion after her mother passed away, but they were nothing like the London house. Before she could get her suitcases unloaded, a loud thumping of the stairs grew louder and louder, and then the door to the room swung open.

"Violet!" Mary Ellen cried out, running up and embracing her long-missed sister. The young women cheered and cried, going on and on about how much they missed each other and everything else they couldn't fit into an envelope.

"Where is that baby boy?" Violet asked, looking over at Margaret, who was holding him near the doorway. "Oh! Come here to your Auntie Violet," she cried out, arms outstretched. Gregory instantly took to her and patted her cheeks with his chubby little hands while giggling and babbling away. Mrs. Parker came back up to the room to let them know a tea had been set out in the back garden for them. The girls enjoyed their tea time snacks, playing with little Gregory, and catching up on the last few years of missing time.

"Tell me about Andre!" Mary Ellen asked, "He must be devastated that you've gone so far away."

"He was working as a cook before the war. Got himself a job at a restaurant in Lafayette and worked his way up to the boss," she said, proudly. "After Momma died, I took a train as far as I could afford to and when I got off, I went and got me a lunch at his restaurant. He needed a waitress and he got himself a wife in the deal." Violet went on about stories from home—what their old friends and neighbors were up to, and who she hadn't seen or heard from since they left the house. After tea, the girls went back inside to change and rest for dinner. Violet took a nap in her room, since her body was still adjusting to the time difference. Knowing they were having a visitor for the week, Thomas came home early from work so he could spend time with the family.

That night at dinner, Violet enjoyed talking with Uncle Edmund and Thomas, who asked her every possible question they could come up with about modern life in reconstructed America—questions that Mary Ellen couldn't have answered. When Edmund said he would have to go eat at her restaurant when he planned to visit America the next year, she said she would be glad to have him over for dinner to repay his hospitality. After their meal, everyone went over to the library for drinks. Normally, only Mary Ellen would go in the library to smoke and have her whiskey, which gave Margaret extra time to set up the room.

"It's so nice to have company after dinner," Mary Ellen said, lighting her pipe with a long matchstick. Violet stood by the fireplace while she looked over the volumes of books along the walls. Thomas, who had taken a little too much wine at dinner and an extra pill, whispered to Mary Ellen, "Does she know how to read?" Mary Ellen elbowed him in the hip, reminding him that they write letters to each other once a month. That night, everyone slept soundly and calmly for the first time in weeks. After taking her to the theatre, a ballet, and a summer market at Trafalgar square, it was time for Violet to go home. Mary Ellen and the baby rode to the train station with her to see her off. Both girls in tears, Mary Ellen promised the next time she would have to come stay at Redbriar. Violet said she would hold Mary Ellen to that promise. As the train left to take her to the harbor, Mary Ellen could feel a sense of dread falling through her chest. She asked the cab driver to take them home quickly, claiming the baby wasn't feeling well.

Once at the house, she could hear shouting and shattering of things from the inside. Mr. Taylor quickly let her in and Mrs. Parker took Gregory upstairs. Thomas was still home, having not gone to work that day, and he was in a frenzy. He had pulled several paintings off the walls of the house and was stamping on them in the hallway.

"Thomas Morgan!" Mary Ellen shouted. "What are you doing!?"

"Fuck you, Mary Ellen, and fuck this house!" he shouted, stabbing a wall with a nearby candelabra.

"You're sick, Thomas! Get control of yourself!" She tried to grab his arms and calm him down. He pushed her to the floor and spat, his hair flying into his face.

Mr. Taylor came up to help and informed Mary Ellen that he had already sent for a constable. Edmund was already at work at the bank, and Mrs. Parker had taken the maids down to the servant's hall and closed the door. Thomas began punching the floorboards, ripping the thin strips up from the ground with his hands, blood dripping from his fingers. "Thomas, stop!" Mary Ellen cried. "Mr. Taylor, do something!"

Mr. Taylor nodded and rushed to tackle Thomas to the ground as he had done before. However, without Edmund's help, he quickly lost control and was soon being pummeled with punches.

"Shit," Mary Ellen said, and dashed up the stairs as fast as she could. Up in her room, Margaret was holding the baby.

"He's lost it Mary Ellen. Just stay up here where it's safe until he burns himself out."

Mary Ellen ran to her desk and pulled out the revolver.

"Come on, just let him break a few dishes. He isn't in his right mind," Margaret said, trying to talk her out of doing anything drastic.

"He is going to kill Mr. Taylor if I don't get down there. Stay here with Gregory. If you don't hear a gunshot, lock the door and wait for the constable," Mary Ellen ordered. Margaret nodded, holding the crying baby.

Mary Ellen hurried downstairs, revolver in her hand, but before she could make it to the parlor, she saw the constable standing at the doorway with a bruised and bloodied Mr. Taylor. Mary Ellen stuffed the gun into her dress pockets and slowly made her way down to them.

"Ah, Mrs. Morgan," the constable said cheerfully. "Everything is fine here. Why don't you head back upstairs." Mr. Taylor nodded to her to agree, and so she did, slowly backing up to her room. From the staircase she could hear Mr. Taylor talking to the policeman. He had come up with a story about a robber who had broken into the house without realizing the lord was still having his breakfast and a fight had broken out. Thomas had been "knocked out" and the criminal had fled before the constable arrived. Once the officer made his report and suggested they call for a doctor, he left the house. Mary Ellen dashed down the stairs to see her husband unconscious on the floor of the hallway. He began to shiver and call out random words. She pulled the gun from her dress and aimed it at him. "Lady Morgan! You mustn't!" he said, rushing over to her.

"He'd done so well," she said, tears running down her face. "It's only going to get worse, Mr. Taylor."

Then Mrs. Parker and the rest of the maids arrived in the parlor. "Lady Murphy, what are you doing with that gun!?" she cried and told her staff to head back to the safety of the kitchen.

"No, keep them in here. I won't have any vile gossip about me running around this house. I'm going to kill this sick beast." Mary Ellen aimed the gun up to his chest. "You're all going to tell the constable the robber came back and shot him." She was stopped by pair of hands coming up behind her, grabbing the gun away. Margaret, having quickly disarmed her, stuffed the gun in her apron and slapped Mary Ellen across the face.

"And you'll be hanged when they realize he was shot with your daddy's American pistol."

Mary Ellen winced, holding her burning cheek. "What do we do then?"

"Well, we don't do it in the middle of bloody police-soaked London."

Mr. Taylor had carried Thomas back upstairs to his room to rest and recover then joined the remainder of the staff and Mary Ellen in the servants' dining area downstairs. Mrs. Parker suggested having him placed in an asylum, but Mary Ellen pointed out that he would need to do so voluntarily or by a doctor's orders. "He is clearly ill, my lady, we can all vouch for this," Mrs. Parker said.

"Then bring shame on the house by having his Lordship in an institution?" Mr. Taylor said. "I'm on Lady Mary Ellen's side of this. He's just beyond help."

Richmond quietly arrived from upstairs. "His habit will end him eventually. If we let him continue, he will surely injure more of us." He rolled up his shirt sleeve to display the bruises on his arms. "I've tried to keep him from taking them before, and he gets violently ill after a few days. I found that a steady amount works for a while, but he gets into these fits where he takes too many at once and, well, he becomes an absolute beast. I'm at a loss as well," he said, sitting down at the table with them. Mary Ellen winced at the sight of Richmond's bruises. Thomas had never physically harmed her until that morning.

"How long have you tried to help him?" Mary Ellen asked.

"He started taking them about four years ago, but only in the last year has he started showing any symptoms," he said. Richmond wasn't one to talk about his employer behind his back but given the circumstances he felt it was necessary.

Mrs. Parker stirred her tea. "But if we can take him to an asylum…"

"Then he will just die there." One of the maids chimed in. Everyone in the room looked over to her. "I was working in houses before where the lady or a son was sent to one, and they only come back in coffins."

"I do hear they are dreadful places, Lady Morgan," another maid said. Now that confidence among the staff was growing, the remainder weighed in on their experiences with the current business of doctors and opium-eating addictions.

Mr. Taylor ended the chatter. "Alright, then. We must make a decision now as for what to do with him." He looked over the room.

"Raise your hand if you wish to have him sent to an institution," Mary Ellen called out. Two maids, the cook, and one of the footmen raised their hands. "Alright then, raise your hands if you wish to return to Redbriar and see to his 'condition' there." The remaining hands went up.

"Does anyone here have a moral objection to this plan?" Edmund asked looking down the table. No one spoke up. "Because if you do, you may stay here and be free of any repercussions should this plan go poorly."

"Will we be let go if we do?" the stable boy asked.

"No, son. And if you wish to leave now, your references will remain positive," Edmund said.

"God don't forgive killin'," the boy said.

"Forgiveness is up to God," Edmund answered.

12

The Aftermath

The next two days were quiet around the London house, even with the staff hurrying to pack the family's things to return to Redbriar for the remainder of the summer. Edmund and his skeleton staff were to stay at the house as per usual, while the rest of the small army went along with family. Thomas had been severely disheartened by his actions that day and had personally apologized to nearly every member of the staff. Mary Ellen and Richmond did their best to keep an eye on him, including when he was taking the pills, when he was lying about taking them, and when he forgot he had already taken them. He stammered when he spoke, and often would repeat himself mid-sentence. "Why are we going back to Redbriar?" he asked, for the third time that hour.

"We are throwing a summer party there next month, remember?" Mary Ellen said, holding little Gregory. She made a point to let Thomas hold him as much as she could from that point on, in hopes that the boy might remember something of his father when he was older. Every time he held him, she felt a sense of dread, and never left Thomas alone with the child. At any moment, he could break into a fit of rage and easily hurt little Gregory. As far as the staff was concerned, no other procedures had changed. Richmond cleaned his shoes and did combed his hair every morning as usual. He handed Thomas his morning, luncheon, and evening pills as he always did.

The trip back to Redbriar was bright and sunny. Their coach had been recently cleaned out, and things just seemed as though everything would be alright, that perhaps he would get better being away from the city and the stress of work. The staff arrived before the family to prepare the house and clean. They had to be careful not to inform the permanent Redbriar staff of their plans, making sure not to speak of things unless they were alone in their private rooms. A date was set, and invitations to come visit for a weekend were sent to a few friends of his as well as Evelin and her husband. There was to be a simple picnic party under cream-colored tents out on the grounds. A small brass band would play, and the children would have ice cream and games. Mary Ellen wanted Thomas to have a few good memories in his final hours, as the plan was that after everyone went home that evening, he would suffer a tragic accident.

However, once back at the estate, Thomas's behavior had spontaneously become erratic. He would hide in one of the many rooms for hours, laughing hysterically as everyone tried to find which one he was in. He would go down to the staff dining room during meal time and ask to eat there—which he was, of course, granted. Mary Ellen found him often writing letters to his friends back in London that included sensational stories of how they kept zebras on the grounds at Redbriar, and how they kept an entire zoo of creatures inside the rooms. She never let these letters leave the house, always offering to have them posted for him. Reading the scrawled text made her cry as she came to terms with the fact that her once loving husband was now clearly going mad. Margaret tried to remind her that they were going to help him soon, that he wouldn't be sick any longer. Most importantly, that nobody was going to be hurt again. His eccentric behavior made it easy to feel sympathy for him, until the memory of how violent his outbursts could be returned. The fear that at any moment he could explode into a fit of rage put most of the house on edge.

After a few weeks of mostly peaceful life, the guests began to arrive for the little summer party. Men from the nearby village were brought over to construct the a tent, the a chef went to work on the food, the a band was given rooms to stay in upstairs, and the sound of their friends' children running up and down the hallways lit up the house. Thomas was in great spirits for the duration of the preparations and was mostly content in his behavior as Richmond had given him a double dose for the days the guests would be there. With a much more stable Thomas showing off the house to his friends, Mary Ellen and Margaret set to work in preparing for the aftermath. They each met with the staff members who were aware of things, telling them where they needed to be and at what time they should head in or out of the house. While they knew he was going to die, they were mostly kept in the dark as to how it would be done. This way, should the police question them about the "accident," they could answer truthfully about not having witnessed it. Margaret was even somewhat in the dark about the final stages but had Mary Ellen promise her that she simply wouldn't walk up and shoot him while he slept. "No, Margaret. Besides, that old gun hasn't been cleaned in so long I doubt it actually fires."

The garden party was a huge success, and even Richmond seemed to be enjoying himself. Thomas danced and played with the children, and wasn't so high as to be unaware of his surroundings.

"Thank you so much for inviting us, Mary Ellen," Evelin said, holding her daughter who had fallen asleep after too much ice cream. "You simply must come visit us soon. Perhaps Lord Morgan would fancy a hunt on our grounds?"

Mary Ellen smiled. "He would enjoy that immensely," she said, her eyes welling up with tears.

That evening, after the band left and their guests headed back to the village to catch the train home, Mary Ellen sat outside on the grounds smoking her pipe. Margaret had taken Gregory upstairs to bed early, having exhausted himself playing outside all day. Thomas was helping the other men tear down the tents while dinner was being prepared inside. Richmond came up behind her and placed his hand on her shoulder. "You've given him one more happy day, Lady Morgan. Let's do this quickly."

She nodded, her eyes still red from earlier in the day. "Alright. Get him upstairs."

Mary Ellen met with Margaret in her room to get dressed for dinner. They had were to have one final meal together, and she wanted to look her best. His She wore his favorite blue dress and had her hair pulled back in a simple bun. He hated elaborate styling on women. She and Margaret headed out to the stairwell and stopped for a moment. "Wait, I want the other gloves."

Margaret went back to the bedroom to get a different pair. Mary Ellen looked over the banister at the massive house below her and worried about what would happen if their plans failed, or they were found out. She and half her staff would be hanged. He could survive, only to be carted away to die in an institution. Their son would be put in the care of his uncle Edmund, never really knowing his parents. She could hear Margaret coming up behind her and sighed.

"I don't know if I can do this," she said, still looking at the ground below her.

Something hard and small pressed against the back of her head, followed by the clacking of a revolver's hammer. Mary Ellen froze in place.

"Margaret?" She slowly turned around to see Thomas standing over her, holding her father's gun to her forehead.

"BANG BANG!" he shouted and burst into laughter. "I found this in your room. Where did you get this old thing?" He waved it around in the air. "It doesn't work though, see," he said, pulling the trigger while still aiming at her. The hammer refused to move. "Damn thing is locked up. You have to oil these things, you know."

Mary Ellen felt a deep pressure in her chest as she fought to catch her breath. Margaret soon came up behind him with her gloves. The look on her face at the sight of him with the gun turned her face as white as her apron.

He turned around and aimed the gun at Margaret. "See, it's just too rusty to fire," he said, pulling the trigger.

It did fire, the sound deafening. Margaret turned around to see where the bullet had gone before recognizing the growing pain in her arm. She looked down to see that part of her sleeve and a mass of flesh and chunk of bone were missing. Then the pain set in. Mary Ellen rushed over to her, blood was now freely running from the wound. Margaret swore, holding her arm with a blood-soaked hand. Mary Ellen took Margaret's waist apron and quickly wrapped it around her shoulder to try and stop the bleeding.

"Oh no, what happened?" Thomas asked, not realizing what he had done. Mary Ellen turned to look at him, her plans now ruined, her life about to be ruined. The gunshot had woken up the baby and staff began collecting downstairs to see what had happened—mostly to see if she was the one who did had done the shooting. Thomas backed up to the banister to see the commotion. He waved to everyone, gun still in his hand, oblivious to the situation. The staff gasped, some rushing away to safety. "It's alright, I just shot Mrs. Harrison. But it's OK, she's is fine," he called out.

Mary Ellen watched him do this, then looked back down at Margaret, who was in tears, her blood soaking the hallway carpet as her jaw began to shake.

Mary Ellen felt an anger burn from her chest into her skull, searing her eyes. She took a deep breath and called out to him.

"Thomas Morgan!"

He turned around to see who had called his name. "Yes?"

She ran toward him and leapt, grabbing him by the shoulders and sent them both tumbling over the banister to the hard ground three flights below. They landed with an abrupt and terrifying sound. The staff that still remained in the room rushed to their aid. Mr. Taylor was first to them, turning a limp Mary Ellen over. She had landed on Thomas in the fall but was unconscious. He tapped her cheeks with his hands.

"Lady Morgan!" he shouted over and over. "Wake up!"

Her eyes slowly opened, and she gasped for air.

Mr. Taylor took her by the hand and helped her sit up on the ground. "Are you alright?"

Mary Ellen looked over at her husband's body beside her. His chest was crushed in the fall and blood was pooling from his mouth and ribs that were now sticking out of his shirt. The impact had killed him instantly.

"No," she replied.

"It was an accident, my lady. Three stories that fall was," Mr. Taylor said standing to help her up.

"He shot her," she said, getting to her feet in an attempt to kick his body, but when she tried to stand, her legs collapsed under her. Mr. Taylor caught her before she could fall.

"Are you sure you're alright?" he asked, the look in her eyes gave him his answer. A footman rushed over to bring a chair for her to sit in. "Can you feel them?" She nodded clenching her teeth through the pain of a broken leg and remained on the floor.

"Get a doctor! Hurry!" she said. Another footman had brought Margaret downstairs in his arms, with her good arm wrapped behind his shoulders. Her face was pale from the blood loss, but the majority of the bleeding had stopped. He sat her down in the chair beside Mary Ellen before helping the rest of the men put a sheet over Thomas's body.

Margaret leaned over and whispered. "That wasn't your plan was it?" Mary Ellen coughed a laugh and reached into her dress pocket. She pulled out her fist and slowly opened it to reveal a small box of fresh, paper-wrapped cartridges.

Several months passed as the estate prepared for Christmas. Margaret was busy in the parlor, helping little Gregory decorate the tree with low hanging ornaments with her remaining arm when Mr. Taylor answered a knock at the door.

"Who is it?" Mary Ellen asked, sitting in her chair and unwrapping ornaments from their protective paper.

"There is a Detective Drake here to see you, Lady Morgan."

"Bring him in then," she said, reaching over for her cane.

The detective introduced himself and apologized for the unannounced visit so close to the holiday.

"I am in town visiting my mother in the village." He removed his hat.

"We've already had several authorities investigate my husband's death, Mr. Drake," she said calmly.

"Yes, I understand, Lady Morgan. I'm actually a friend of your uncle's," he said, handing her a heavy package wrapped in brown butcher paper. "Thought you might light to have this back where it belongs."

"Why thank you, detective. I didn't think I would see it again." She opened the paper to reveal her father's revolver. "Would you like to stay for tea?"

"Perhaps another time. I was at your uncle's investigating the discovery of a young boy found in a canal. Turns out he was a stable boy that went missing a few days after your family left the house," he said, watching Mary Ellen pull her pipe from her pocket.

"Well, London is a dangerous place, Mr. Drake," she said, lighting it. "It's a shame, really."

"Aye, Miss. A shame." He replaced his hat. "Between us, it would be best if your family stayed here at Redbriar until things return to normal."

Mary Ellen smiled. "Thank you, Detective Drake."

He smiled and tipped his hat. "Happy Christmas, Baroness."

"Merry Christmas."

www.ingramcontent.com/pod-product-compliance
Lightning Source LLC
Chambersburg PA
CBHW050143110726
47898CB00008B/2650